LOST

IN

LITIGATION

(A JOURNEY OF A FIRST-GENERATION LAWYER)

Lost in Litigation

(A Journey of a First-generation Lawyer)

Copyright © 2025 by Lucky Singh

First Printing, 2025

Dedicated

To

My Mummy & Papa, for your endless love and sacrifices.

To

My Didi, my angel, you are my strength and Inspiration.

To

My Bro, whom I've never met but hope to see one day.

This book is for you all.

With love,

Lucky Singh

<u>Acknowledgement</u>

This novel **"Lost in Litigation"** is very close to my heart and bears glimpses of my life, of what I experienced, of what I observed, a few random stories I heard and the several lessons I learned.

There were various people who contributed towards this, some known and some unknown.

Few people who don't even know that they have enriched my life, my thoughts and this story.

They all can't 'be named but they sure can be thanked.

First, **My Parents** for their everlasting support and encouragement. Their blessing and trust gave me the courage to write this novel.

My sister Priya for their constant motivation and encouragement, which helped me to stay focused and driven.

My brother Dimpu & Friend Satvik also deserve special mention for their continuous motivation and support, which played a significant role in helping me complete this novel.

Last but definitely not the least**, My Bro Pranav** for being there for everything, whose presence in my life has been a blessing. His existence has been a source of inspiration and strength for me, and I am grateful for the positive impact he has had on my life, even from a distance.

Thank you.

<u>Chapter 1</u>

The crowded courtroom hummed with murmurs as lawyers paced, clerks shuffled papers, and clients exchanged nervous glances. It was Charu's first case—nothing major, just a simple bail hearing.

Yet, for her, it felt like stepping onto a battlefield.

Dressed in her freshly ironed black coat, she clutched her case file tightly, her palms slightly sweaty. The senior advocates sat in their usual spots, exuding confidence, some barely noticing the young, unfamiliar face among them.

As she waited for her turn, a deep voice broke her thoughts.

"First case?"

Charu turned to see a middle-aged lawyer smirking at her.

Advocate Sinha—a man known for his sharp tongue and even sharper connections.

"Yes, sir," she replied politely.

He chuckled. "Welcome to reality, young lady. Courts are not for dreamers. Hope you survive."

Before Charu could respond, the judge entered, and everyone rose.

"Next case," the clerk announced. "Bail plea for Rajiv Mehta."

Charu inhaled deeply. *This is it.* She walked towards the podium, feeling the weight of a hundred eyes on her.

"Your Honor, my client has been falsely accused—"

Before she could finish, the opposing lawyer, Advocate Bhardwaj, a senior advocate with decades of experience, interrupted.

"Your Honor, this junior counsel is wasting the court's time." He smirked. "She should learn how bail hearings work before arguing."

A few lawyers chuckled. Charu felt her face heat up, but she stood firm.

"Your Honor, I may be new, but I know the law." She lifted her case file. "I have precedent and valid grounds for bail. If the opposing counsel is done with personal remarks, may I continue?"

The judge raised an eyebrow. The murmurs in the room ceased. Advocate Bhardwaj's smirk faded. "Proceed," the judge said, intrigued.

Charu cleared her throat, suppressing her nerves. She laid out her arguments with precision, citing legal precedents, countering every objection Bhardwaj threw her way. By the time she finished, even the court clerks were listening intently.

The judge glanced at Bhardwaj. "Anything to counter?"

Bhardwaj hesitated. He wasn't expecting a fight. "No, Your Honor."

The judge turned to Charu. "Bail granted."

For a moment, silence filled the courtroom. Then, a slow murmur began—whispers of admiration, of surprise. Charu exhaled, a smile tugging at her lips.

As she stepped out, Advocate Sinha caught up to her.

"Not bad, Miss First-Generation." He gave her a half-smile. "Let's see how long you last."

Charu didn't reply. She had won her first battle, but the war had just begun.

Chapter 2

Gaya, Bihar – 2012

The small classroom buzzed with whispers as the teacher wrote "What do you want to be when you grow up?" on the blackboard. Charu, a 14-year-old girl with bright eyes and a sharp mind, didn't hesitate. She quickly scribbled "Lawyer" in her notebook.

Her elder sister, Anu, sitting beside her, glanced at it and sighed.

"Change it," she whispered.

Charu frowned. "Why?"

Anu didn't answer. The bell rang, and the students rushed out, but Charu followed Anu, pressing for a response. "Didi, you always wanted to be a lawyer too. You told me so!"

Anu smiled, but it didn't reach her eyes. "Some dreams aren't meant to be, Charu."

That evening, as they sat in their small two-room house, their mother prepared dinner while their father read the newspaper. Charu, still restless from the conversation, leaned closer to Anu.

"Tell me, Didi. Why didn't you become a lawyer?"

Anu stirred her tea, lost in thought. "Because being the first in a profession is the hardest, Charu. There's no one to guide you, no one to support you. You have to fight every step of the way."

"So?" Charu challenged. "That's what makes it exciting!"

Anu chuckled, brushing a strand of hair behind her ear. "You're still a kid. You don't understand. I had responsibilities—taking care of you, helping Maa, and running the house. And even if I had studied law, who would have given me a chance? Clients only trust those with experience, and judges favor lawyers from big families. First-generation lawyers struggle, Charu. Some don't even survive in the profession."

Charu's hands clenched into fists. "That's unfair!"

Anu smiled sadly. "That's reality."

That night, Charu lay awake, staring at the ceiling. Her sister had given up her dream, but Charu refused to do the same. If the system was unfair, she would fight it. If first-generation lawyers struggled, she would prove they could win.

She didn't know how yet. But she knew one thing—she would become a lawyer. And she would succeed.

The battle had already begun.

Chapter 3

Gaya, Bihar – 2018

The air was thick with the smell of old books and ink as Charu sat in the cramped study room, flipping through her CLAT (Common Law Admission Test) preparation book. The glow of the dim tube light barely reached the corners of the room, but she didn't care.

Her dreams burned brighter than any light.

Anu entered with a cup of tea and placed it in front of her. "Take a break, Charu. You've been studying for hours."

Charu didn't look up. "I don't have time for breaks, Didi. CLAT is tough. If I crack it, I can get into a good law college."

Anu sat down beside her, watching her little sister's determination. "And if you don't?"

Charu finally looked up, her eyes fierce. "Then I'll try again. And again. I won't stop until I get in."

Anu smiled but said nothing. She saw the fire in Charu's eyes—the same fire she once had. But life had extinguished hers. She prayed the world wouldn't do the same to Charu.

The Argument That Changed Everything

One evening, their father walked into the house, tired from a long day at work. Charu hesitated but then spoke up. "Papa, I want to study law. I need to go to a good college."

Her father looked at her, then at Anu. "Law? Do you know how difficult it is? You have no connections, Charu. No one will help you. Look at Anu—she's smart too, but she didn't waste her time on impossible dreams."

Anu looked down, while Charu's hands clenched into fists. "It's not impossible, Papa. I'll work hard."

Her father sighed. "And what if you fail? What if after five years, you don't get a single case? What will you do then?"

Charu stood up, her heart pounding. "Then I'll create my own path! Someone has to start, Papa. If I become a lawyer, the next generation in our family won't struggle like me. Someone has to take the first step."

For a moment, there was silence. Then, her father looked at Anu. "Talk some sense into her."

Anu hesitated, then did something unexpected—she placed a hand on Charu's shoulder. "Let her try, Papa. Maybe she'll succeed where I couldn't."

Her father looked between his daughters, sighed deeply, and nodded. "Fine. But remember, Charu—this road is tough. If you give up halfway, don't come crying to me."

Charu's lips curled into a determined smile. "I won't give up.
Ever."

Months passed in a blur of books, mock tests, and sleepless nights.
On the day of the CLAT results, Charu's hands shook as she
refreshed the page on her old phone.
AIR 432 (All India Rank)

She screamed. Anu ran into the room. "What happened?"
Charu turned, eyes shining with tears. "I did it, Didi. I got into
MIT-WPU, Pune!"
Anu hugged her tight, her voice choking. "I'm so proud of you,
Charu."
But as Charu packed her bags for Pune, she didn't know that this
was just the first victory. The real battle—against nepotism,
injustice, and survival in the courtroom—was yet to come.
And she was ready.

<u>Chapter 4</u>

Pune – 2018

The sprawling campus of MIT-WPU stood before Charu like a different world—grand buildings, manicured lawns, and students confidently discussing legal theories as if they had been born into the profession.

Clutching her admission papers, Charu inhaled deeply. This is it. The first step toward becoming a lawyer.

First Day, First Shock

Inside the lecture hall, students were introducing themselves.

"Hi, I'm Raghav Mehta. My father is a High Court judge."

"I'm Sneha Sharma. My grandfather was a Supreme Court lawyer."

"I'm Abhishek Verma. My uncle owns the biggest law firm in Delhi."

When Charu's turn came, she stood up and said, "I'm Charu from Gaya, Bihar. First-generation law student."

Silence. A few exchanged glances; some smirked. She could almost hear their thoughts: *No connections? No chance.*

After class, as she walked to the library, a girl stopped her. "You're from Bihar?" she asked, raising an eyebrow. "Are there even courts there?"

Charu's blood boiled, but she forced a smile. "Yes. And some of the greatest lawyers and judges have come from Bihar. You'll read about them soon."

The girl scoffed and walked away. Charu clenched her fists. *So, this is how they see me?*

A month later, Charu applied for an internship at a reputed law firm. The interview went well—until the partner asked, "Who in your family is in the legal profession?"

"No one," she replied.

The man exchanged a knowing look with his colleague. "We prefer candidates with a legal background. They understand the system better."

Charu walked out, rejection letter in hand. The lesson was clear: *Knowledge isn't enough. In law, connections matter more than merit.*

That night, she called Anu. "Didi, they don't take us seriously. They think we don't belong."

Anu's voice was gentle yet firm. "Then prove them wrong, Charu. Make them see you."

Determined, Charu started reading extra cases, volunteering for moot courts, and joining legal aid programs. She knew she couldn't rely on her surname, so she built her reputation with hard work.

One day, a high-profile moot court competition was announced. The winner would get a direct internship with a Supreme Court lawyer. Charu signed up.

When her name was announced, a few students whispered, "Let's see how a first-gen lawyer competes with us."

Charu smiled. *They'll see soon enough.*

This competition wasn't just about winning. It was about proving that first-generation lawyers *deserved* a place in the courtroom.

The battle had begun.

<u>Chapter 5</u>

The auditorium was packed. The moot court competition was no ordinary event—judges from real courts, senior advocates, and legal professors sat as panellists. The winner would secure an internship with a Supreme Court lawyer, a golden opportunity for any aspiring advocate.

Charu stood outside the hall, breathing deeply. She had spent weeks preparing, researching case laws, structuring arguments, and rehearsing her speech. But nerves crept in as she saw her competitors—students from legal families, some even mentored by judges.

A familiar voice broke her thoughts. "Nervous?"

She turned to see Aniket, a classmate who had always been neutral toward her.

"Excited," she corrected him.

He smirked. "I hope you're ready. Raghav is in the final round too. His dad's a High Court judge, and he's been trained in advocacy since childhood."

Charu smiled. "Good. Let him watch how self-made lawyers argue."

Inside, the first few rounds went as expected—some participants stammered, some were overconfident, and some delivered polished arguments. Charu, however, remained focused.

When her turn came, she adjusted her black coat and walked to the podium.

The judge asked, "Counsel, are you ready?"

"Yes, My Lord," she said firmly.

The case was about a corporate fraud scandal. Charu presented her arguments clearly, citing relevant precedents, and countering the opposing counsel with confidence.

Then came the hardest part—the rebuttal.

Raghav stood up, smirking. "Your argument is based on an outdated precedent, Counsel. The Supreme Court overruled it in 2014."

Some students chuckled. Charu felt her heart pound, but she quickly regained composure.

"With due respect, My Lord, my learned friend is mistaken. The 2014 judgment modified the application, but it did not overrule the core principle. If I may direct the court to Paragraph 17 of the judgment…" She paused, then looked directly at Raghav. "Perhaps my opponent should read the case fully before making assumptions."

A few gasps echoed in the hall. Even the judges raised their eyebrows.

Raghav sat down, clearly embarrassed.

Victory & Realization

After all rounds concluded, the judges announced the results.

"The winner of the moot court competition is… Charu Mishra!"

Applause filled the room, but Charu barely heard it. She had done it.

As she walked out, Raghav stopped her. "You got lucky."

She smirked. "No, I got prepared."

That night, she called Anu. "Didi, I won!"

Anu's voice cracked with emotion. "I knew you would. You're breaking the barriers I was afraid of, Charu."

But as Charu celebrated, she knew this was just the beginning.

Winning a moot court was one thing—surviving in the real courtroom was another.

And the real battles were yet to come.

Chapter 6

Charu's victory in the moot court competition had earned her an internship with a reputed Supreme Court lawyer, Advocate S.K. Mehra. It was her first step into the real world of litigation.

Charu arrived at Mehra's office, a grand setup with tall wooden bookshelves and walls decorated with framed newspaper articles about landmark cases. She adjusted her bag and took a deep breath before stepping inside.
The receptionist barely looked at her. "Interns sit in that corner. Don't disturb anyone."
Charu nodded and walked toward the designated area, where a few other interns were already working. One of them, a tall guy in a crisp white shirt, smirked.
"First time in a law firm?" he asked.
"Yes," Charu replied, placing her bag down.
"You'll mostly be making coffee and organizing case files," he chuckled.
Charu didn't respond. *If I have to start at the bottom, I will. But I won't stay here forever.*

A week later, Charu got the opportunity to visit the High Court with Advocate Mehra. It was nothing like the moot court—here, the atmosphere was chaotic yet controlled. Senior advocates walked with an air of confidence, clerks ran around with case files, and junior lawyers stood waiting for their turn to argue.

As they entered the courtroom, Mehra turned to Charu. "Observe everything. Learn not just from the arguments but from the way lawyers conduct themselves."

Charu nodded, gripping her notepad tightly.

The case was about corporate fraud, similar to her moot court competition, but this time, it wasn't a simulation. The opposing lawyer, an experienced senior, attacked every argument Mehra presented. Charu watched closely, noting how Mehra remained calm, responding with precise counterpoints.

During a break, Mehra asked Charu, "What did you learn?"

Charu thought for a moment. "That facts alone don't win a case. It's about how you present them."

Mehra smiled. "Good. You have potential, but potential isn't enough. You need resilience. Most first-generation lawyers quit before they make it. Will you?"

Charu met his gaze. "Never."

Back at the office, Mehra handed Charu a thick file. "Draft a legal reply for this case by tomorrow morning."

Charu's eyes widened. "Tomorrow?"

"If you can't handle this, how will you survive in the profession?" he said, walking away.

That night, Charu stayed in the office, reading through the case papers. She struggled, making mistakes, erasing and rewriting. By 3 AM, she finally completed the draft.

The next morning, she nervously handed it to Mehra. He scanned through it, then looked up. "Not bad. Needs refinement, but you did better than expected."

A rush of pride filled Charu, but she kept her expression neutral. *One small victory. Many more to come.*

One afternoon, Charu overheard a conversation in the office.

"Why did Mehra Sir give Charu the drafting task? She's not from a legal family."

"Exactly. We've been here longer, but she wins one moot court, and suddenly she's special?"

Charu felt a pang of anger but didn't react. Instead, she worked harder.

Mehra noticed her dedication. "Good work, Charu. I'll let you assist me in a real case next week."

This was it—her first real case. But she had no idea that it would test her patience, strength, and everything she believed in.

Chapter 7

A week later, Charu's moment arrived. She was assigned to assist Advocate Mehra in a wrongful termination case. The client, Mr. Ramesh Tiwari, had been fired from a reputed firm without proper notice or compensation.

Mehra handed Charu the case file. "You'll draft the opening statement and assist in research. Read everything carefully."

Charu's heart pounded. This wasn't an internship task—this was real.

Charu stayed up all night studying similar cases and legal provisions. She drafted the opening statement, ensuring it was crisp, persuasive, and backed by precedent.

The next morning, she presented it to Mehra.

He skimmed through it, then raised an eyebrow. "Not bad, but…"

He circled a paragraph. "This part is weak. Your argument should have more weight. Never give the opposition a chance to punch holes in your case."

Charu nodded and rewrote it, determined to get it right.

The next day, Charu entered the courtroom as part of Mehra's team. This time, she wasn't an observer—she was a participant.

The opposing counsel was Advocate Sandeep Khanna, a well-known senior lawyer. He exuded confidence, his voice commanding respect.

As Mehra presented the case, Khanna smirked. "My Lords, this is a clear case of an employee failing to meet performance expectations. The company followed due process."

Charu clenched her fists. She knew this wasn't true. She leaned toward Mehra and whispered, "Sir, Clause 14 in the company's HR manual contradicts this. They were required to give a three-month warning."

Mehra glanced at her, then turned back to the judge. "My Lords, let's look at Clause 14 of the company's policy, which my learned friend seems to have overlooked."

The judge read the document and frowned. "Mr. Khanna, do you have a response?"

Khanna stammered, flipping through his notes. "My Lords, I… uh…"

Charu held her breath.

The judge finally spoke. "It appears the termination was unjustified. The court rules in favour of Mr. Tiwari. Compensation will be granted."

Charu's heart raced. *We won!*

As they walked out, Mehra patted her back. "Good job, Charu. That detail turned the case in our favour."

That night, Charu called Anu.

"Didi, I helped win a case today!" she said, excitement bubbling in her voice.

Anu chuckled. "I'm so proud of you, Charu. But remember, this is just one battle. Many more are waiting for you."

Charu smiled. "I know, Didi. And I'm ready for all of them."

Little did she know, the biggest challenge of her legal career was about to begin—a case that would shake the foundations of her belief in justice.

<u>Chapter 8</u>

A few months had passed since Charu's first victory in the wrongful termination case. She had gained confidence, and her relationship with Mehra had grown stronger. He began trusting her with more responsibilities, which included attending client meetings, drafting legal documents, and even speaking during certain hearings.

But the real challenge came one afternoon, when Mehra handed her a new case file.

"Charu, this case needs someone sharp and unafraid to stand up for what's right," Mehra said, pushing a thick folder toward her. "I think you're ready."

Charu opened the folder and skimmed through the details. It was a rape case, but not one she had ever expected to be handling. The accused was a well-known politician, and the victim was a young woman from a poor family who had come forward with the accusation.

Charu looked up at Mehra, her heart pounding. "This… this is huge, Sir. Are you sure I should be working on this?"

Mehra leaned back in his chair. "It's the cases that scare you the most that test you the hardest. If you truly want to make a difference, Charu, you'll have to fight for justice, no matter the consequences."

Charu felt the weight of his words. This was not just any case—it was one that could make or break her career. The media attention, the political pressure, the possibility of failure…

But she had no choice. Her sense of justice burned within her.

The case quickly became the talk of the town. Every newspaper, every TV channel, and every social media feed buzzed with the story of the young woman accusing the politician. Charu found herself surrounded by debates, public opinions, and judgments, even before the case had gone to court.

The victim, Rina, was a college student from a village near Pune. She had been working as a part-time maid at the politician's house, and she claimed the assault had occurred when she had gone there to do some cleaning. The politician, on the other hand, denied all accusations, stating that it was a political ploy to ruin his career.

Charu attended the initial hearings with Mehra, where the pressure was evident. The courtroom was filled with reporters, and the judge struggled to keep the proceedings calm. The opposing counsel was a powerful lawyer, one who was close to the politician and had an arsenal of tactics at his disposal.

At one point, Charu stood to present evidence. She had meticulously gathered witness testimonies and medical reports, all supporting Rina's claims. As she laid out the evidence before the court, she could feel the stares from the gallery.

"This evidence is flawed," the opposing counsel interjected. "The witness testimonies are unreliable, and the medical report is inconclusive. My client is being framed."

Charu clenched her fists but maintained her composure. "The truth is not swayed by the powerful. Justice must be blind to fame and money."

But even as she spoke, she knew the stakes were high. The media was quick to label the case, and Rina's credibility was being questioned at every turn.

As the trial continued, Charu faced unexpected pressure. Late one evening, she received a call from an unknown number.

"Ms. Charu, this is Ajay Malhotra. I have connections in high places, and I suggest you drop this case. It's getting too messy, and you're a young lawyer. You don't want to jeopardize your career over something like this."

Charu felt the chill in his voice. "What exactly are you threatening me with?"

Ajay laughed, his voice dripping with sarcasm. "Not threatening, just advising. Think carefully."

Charu slammed the phone down, feeling a rush of anger and fear. The system was corrupt, and it was clear that the powerful were trying to silence her. But giving up was never an option for Charu.

The case reached a critical juncture when Mehra fell ill and couldn't attend one of the key hearings. Charu was left to represent the entire case on her own. She felt a sense of both fear and empowerment.

The court session began, and the opposing counsel made his usual aggressive statements, trying to cast doubt on Rina's testimony. The defense had almost convinced the court that the victim's accusations were politically motivated.

Charu stood up, her heart racing but her resolve stronger than ever. "My Lord, I respectfully submit that no political figure, however influential, should be above the law. What we have here is a woman's voice, a cry for justice. And it is our duty to hear it, not silence it."

Her words rang out, echoing in the silent courtroom. She continued to present new evidence, including a crucial phone record that linked the accused to the crime scene on the day Rina had been assaulted.

For the first time in the trial, the judge seemed to take notice. "The court will deliberate. We will reconvene tomorrow."

That night, Charu stayed awake, staring at the file in front of her. She knew the final decision was coming soon. But she had done everything she could—she had fought for the truth, for Rina, and for justice.

The next day, Charu returned to court with a sense of trepidation. The judge had reserved the judgment for that afternoon.

When the verdict was finally delivered, the courtroom was tense. The judge cleared his throat before speaking.

"After careful deliberation, the court has found the defendant guilty of the charges. The politician will face legal consequences for his actions, and the victim shall receive the justice she deserves."

The courtroom erupted in applause from Rina's supporters. Charu stood frozen for a moment, unable to fully process what had just happened.

Rina's mother hugged her, tears streaming down her face. "Thank you… Thank you for everything."

Charu felt a rush of relief, but also a deep sadness for the long road ahead for Rina. The battle had been won, but the fight for justice never truly ended.

As Charu left the courtroom, she felt the weight of the case lift off her shoulders. She had taken on the powerful, fought through the corruption, and won. But she knew this case would haunt her forever, for it had opened her eyes to the reality of law—how fragile justice could be in a world governed by power and influence.

Mehra walked up to her, a rare smile on his face. "Well done, Charu. You passed the ultimate test."

Charu looked at him, her voice steady. "This is just the beginning, Sir. There are many more cases, and I'm ready for every single one of them."

And so, Charu's journey as a first-generation lawyer continued—one victory, one challenge, and one battle at a time

Chapter 9

Charu's reputation as a fierce advocate for justice was growing, but with each victory came new challenges. She had just completed the high-profile rape case, which had garnered significant media attention. Despite the relief she felt from that success, she was acutely aware that her journey was far from over.

One afternoon, Mehra called her into his office with a new case—a corporate fraud case involving a multinational company accused of embezzling millions of rupees. The case was as complicated as it was risky, and Charu could already feel the weight of it on her shoulders.

"Charu," Mehra began, his tone serious. "This is going to be a tough one. The company is well-connected, and the accused executives have powerful allies. But I believe you have what it takes."

Charu nodded, her mind racing. Corporate fraud was a different kind of beast. The stakes were high, and the power dynamics were more complex than she had ever encountered. But she knew she couldn't back down.

"I'm ready, Sir," she said, determination evident in her voice.

The case centered around EverTech Industries, a tech giant with branches in multiple countries. The allegations were that senior executives had siphoned off funds by inflating expenses, creating fake invoices, and falsifying financial records.

Charu started her research, sifting through mountains of financial documents. It was overwhelming, but she knew she had to find the needle in the haystack. The fraud had been happening for years, and the company had covered it up well.

Late one evening, Charu discovered a discrepancy in the accounting ledgers. The same invoice appeared twice, each with a different amount. The amounts were small, but the frequency of the discrepancies suggested a pattern. Charu's heart skipped a beat as she realized the depth of the fraud. This was the breakthrough they needed.

She immediately informed Mehra, who was impressed by her attention to detail. "Good work, Charu. This could be the beginning of cracking the case wide open."

As the trial date approached, Charu prepared for her first confrontation with the opposing counsel. The defense team for EverTech was formidable, led by Vikram Shah, a senior partner at one of the most prestigious law firms in the city.

Shah was smooth, calculated, and far more experienced than Charu. He wasted no time in trying to intimidate her. In the first meeting, he smirked as he extended his hand.

"Ms. Charu, I've heard a lot about you. I must admit, I'm curious to see how a fresh lawyer like you handles this."

Charu forced a smile, not allowing his words to rattle her. "I'll handle it the same way any lawyer should—by focusing on the facts."

Shah raised an eyebrow. "Oh, I'm sure. But when the facts start to change, I wonder how you'll handle that."

His words were a thinly veiled threat, but Charu was determined not to be intimidated. She had come too far to back down now.

The day of the trial arrived, and Charu walked into the courtroom with Mehra by her side. The defense team, led by Vikram Shah, was already seated. The courtroom buzzed with tension. The press had caught wind of the case, and the media was present, eager to see how this high-profile trial would unfold.

Charu began by presenting the evidence of the fraudulent invoices. The documents were clear and irrefutable. But Shah wasn't about to let Charu have an easy victory.

"Your Honor, these invoices are not proof of fraud. They are merely administrative errors," Shah argued. "This is nothing more than a misunderstanding."

Charu stood her ground. "Your Honor, these discrepancies are not just administrative errors. They are part of a larger pattern of embezzlement. The financial records have been tampered with to hide the truth."

Shah smirked. "And how do you propose to prove that? On what basis do you make such a serious accusation?"

Charu felt the weight of his question. She had to be strategic. "I propose we conduct an independent forensic audit of the company's financials. We have already identified irregularities, but a forensic audit will uncover the full extent of the fraud."

The judge looked thoughtful for a moment before nodding. "The court will approve the request for a forensic audit."

Charu's heart skipped a beat. She had won the first round, but the battle was far from over.

Over the next few weeks, the forensic audit revealed shocking findings. The amount of money siphoned off by the executives was staggering—over 50 million rupees had been misappropriated. It was clear that this wasn't just a few errors; it was a well-organized fraud scheme that had been ongoing for years.

The audit results were presented in court, and the defense had no choice but to acknowledge the scale of the fraud. But Vikram Shah wasn't done. He still had a few tricks up his sleeve.

"Your Honor," Shah began, his voice calm but confident. "While it is true that there were discrepancies, there is no evidence to suggest that the senior executives were directly involved in the fraudulent activity. These were isolated actions, and the company itself is not culpable."

Charu knew Shah was trying to divert attention away from the individuals responsible. She leaned forward and addressed the court. "Your Honor, the evidence clearly shows that the executives were not only aware of the fraud, but they actively participated in it. They manipulated the financial records, and they funneled money to their personal accounts. This was not an isolated incident. This was a conspiracy at the highest level of the company."

The courtroom fell silent. Charu had made her point clear.

After weeks of intense legal battles, the judge finally delivered the verdict. "The court finds the executives of EverTech Industries guilty of embezzlement and conspiracy. They will face legal consequences, and the company will be required to pay restitution to the affected parties."

Charu felt a wave of relief wash over her. They had won.

As the court session ended, Mehra turned to Charu with a proud smile. "Well done, Charu. You've handled yourself brilliantly. This case was bigger than you thought, but you didn't back down. You're no longer just a first-generation lawyer. You're a force to be reckoned with."

Charu smiled, her heart swelling with pride. She had proven herself not just to the court, but to herself.

"Thank you, Sir. This is just the beginning."

And as Charu walked out of the courtroom, she knew that the path ahead would be filled with even greater challenges. But now, she was ready.

Chapter 10

Charu's success in the corporate fraud case had garnered attention from all corners of the legal world. Her name was beginning to surface in conversations about rising stars in the legal community. But with fame came pressure, and Charu had learned that the higher you rise, the steeper the fall if you falter.

One morning, as Charu was reviewing her case files in her office, her phone buzzed with an unexpected call. The name on the screen made her pause—Vikram Kapoor, the high-profile political leader who had been implicated in a corruption scandal. Charu had heard of him, but this was the first time he was directly contacting her.

"Ms. Charu, I've heard about your skills," Vikram's voice echoed through the phone. "I need you to represent me in court."

Charu's heart skipped a beat. A case involving a powerful politician could make or break her career, but it also came with risks she had to carefully consider.

"Mr. Kapoor, I need more details about the case before I can make a decision."

"Of course," he replied, his tone smooth and calculated. "Let's meet."

Charu met Vikram Kapoor at his luxurious mansion, a far cry from the modest offices she was used to. The grandeur of the place almost made her feel out of place, but she quickly reminded herself that this was just another challenge to overcome.

Vikram, impeccably dressed in a designer suit, greeted her with a firm handshake. "Ms. Charu, I'm in a difficult spot. I've been accused of accepting bribes and misusing government funds. The media is eating me alive, and I need someone who can fight back."

Charu's mind was racing. Politicians were notoriously hard to defend, especially when public opinion was so strongly against them. But she had made a name for herself by taking on the toughest cases, and this was no different.

"I understand the gravity of the situation, Mr. Kapoor," Charu said, trying to keep her emotions in check. "I need to go through all the evidence before making any commitment, but if I take this case, I will be fighting for the truth, whatever that may be."

Vikram nodded. "That's exactly what I need, Ms. Charu. A lawyer who isn't afraid to fight."

Charu's initial investigation into the case was nothing short of shocking. The accusations were serious—bribes, misuse of public funds, and the creation of fake companies to funnel money into private accounts. On top of that, Vikram's political rivals were eager to see him fall, using every opportunity to tarnish his reputation.

Charu spent days poring over documents, cross-referencing bank records, and meeting with whistleblowers who had once worked with Vikram's team. Slowly, she began to notice discrepancies in the evidence. While there were clear signs of corruption, the prosecution's case seemed too perfect, too well-constructed. She began to suspect that there was more to the story than met the eye. One night, after hours of working, Charu received a call from an anonymous source. "There's more to the case than you think," the voice said. "Vikram's being set up."

Charu's heart pounded in her chest. She asked the source for details, but the line went dead before they could explain further. Was Vikram innocent, or was this just a clever ploy to get her on his side? Charu knew she had to tread carefully.

When the case finally went to trial, Charu was ready. She had uncovered a web of lies and deceit surrounding the allegations, but she also knew the risks of defending a man like Vikram Kapoor. His political connections and public image made the case a political hotbed, and the media was eager for a scandal.

In the courtroom, Vikram sat beside Charu, his usually confident demeanor replaced by nervousness. Charu could feel the weight of the nation's expectations on her shoulders.

The prosecution began by laying out their case: a detailed timeline of Vikram accepting bribes, falsifying documents, and misappropriating government funds. It was a damning case, and the media covered every minute of it. Charu couldn't help but feel the pressure mounting.

"Ms. Charu," the lead prosecutor sneered, "are you seriously suggesting that your client is innocent? The evidence is overwhelming."

Charu stood up, her voice steady. "I am suggesting that the evidence, as it stands, has been manipulated. What you fail to mention, Counsel, is that the so-called 'bribe money' was transferred through a shell company—one that was set up by Vikram's political rivals to frame him."

The courtroom gasped. Charu had just turned the tables.

"Your Honor, we have uncovered that the funds were never transferred into Mr. Kapoor's account," Charu continued, pointing to the financial records on the screen behind her. "They were funneled through an intermediary account, one that had nothing to do with my client."

The defense was starting to make headway, but the prosecution wasn't going to go down without a fight. Vikram's rivals, the people who had orchestrated the smear campaign against him, had far-reaching power and influence.

"Ms. Charu," the prosecutor interrupted, "this is nothing but a baseless conspiracy theory. There is no evidence to back your claims."

Charu shot back with unwavering confidence. "There's plenty of
evidence, but you're too focused on trying to bury the truth. I've
only just begun to uncover the real story."
The case raged on for weeks, each side gaining and losing ground
in the court of public opinion. The media's scrutiny was relentless,
but Charu refused to back down.

As Charu continued her defense, an unexpected twist emerged.
One of Vikram's political rivals—Anjali Reddy, a former associate
who had once worked closely with him—decided to testify. She
revealed that she had been the one to orchestrate the fake
companies and create the fraudulent records to frame Vikram.
"I did it," Anjali confessed in court. "I framed Vikram because he
was about to expose the corruption within our own party. I thought
if I brought him down, I could control the party's future."
Charu's heart raced as the courtroom fell into stunned silence. This
was the break she needed. Vikram's innocence was now beyond
question.

After weeks of tense deliberation, the judge delivered the verdict:
Vikram Kapoor was acquitted of all charges. The political rivals
who had set him up were arrested and charged with conspiracy.
Vikram stood up, visibly relieved. "Charu, you did it. You saved
me."

Charu smiled but remained composed. "I didn't save you, Mr. Kapoor. I just did my job. The truth always comes out in the end."

With the victory behind her, Charu realized that this case had been a turning point in her career. She had faced the biggest challenge of her life and had come out on top, but it wasn't just the win that mattered. It was the knowledge that she had remained true to her principles, even when the odds were stacked against her.

As Charu walked out of the courtroom, she knew the road ahead would continue to be difficult, but she was no longer just a young, inexperienced lawyer trying to prove herself. She was now a force to be reckoned with in the legal world.

And as for the political world? Charu had learned one thing for certain: there would always be corruption, but as long as she stood for the truth, she would never lose the fight.

Chapter 11

The victory in Vikram Kapoor's case had propelled Charu into the spotlight, but it also brought with it an unexpected shift in her personal life. As her career took off, her family's expectations grew heavier. Charu had always been a devoted daughter and sister, but now, the pressure to settle down seemed more insistent than ever. One evening, as Charu sat in her office reviewing case files for an upcoming corporate fraud trial, her phone buzzed. The caller ID showed Dimpu—her younger brother. Charu smiled, knowing that Dimpu's calls were always filled with updates about their family's life.

"Didi, have you thought about what we discussed last time?" Dimpu's voice came through the line, sounding unusually serious.

"Dimpu, I'm busy with a few cases right now. What is it?" Charu asked, leaning back in her chair.

"It's about marriage. The whole family's talking about it. You know, they want you to settle down. You've been working so hard. Maybe it's time to think about your personal life too."

Charu sighed, feeling the weight of the conversation. Marriage had always been a sensitive subject in her family. Her parents, especially her mother, were eager to see her marry, but Charu had always kept her focus on her career, certain that this was her calling.

"Dimpu, I'm not ready. My career means everything to me right now. I don't have the time for all that."

"But Didi, you can't avoid it forever. Mom's worried. She keeps asking when you'll come back home. I know you're busy, but…" Dimpu's voice faltered. "It's hard seeing you alone all the time."

Charu felt a pang of guilt. She knew her family loved her and only wanted what was best for her, but she also knew that their idea of what was best didn't always align with her own dreams. She had fought too hard to get where she was now.

"Dimpu, I promise, we'll talk about this later. But right now, I need to focus on my work."

As the conversation ended, Charu sat in silence, contemplating the words her brother had said. She had always been the ambitious one in the family, the one who chose the difficult path, the one who didn't fit the mold. But now, the family's persistent reminders of her "duty" to settle down were beginning to wear on her.

Later that evening, Charu met Satvik, her close friend and one of the few people who truly understood the balance she struggled with between family and career. Satvik had been Charu's sounding board for years, offering both motivation and wisdom when she felt lost or uncertain.

"You're looking tired, Charu. What's on your mind?" Satvik asked as they sat at their usual spot at a quiet café, a place where Charu could escape the pressure of the legal world for a few hours. Charu didn't hesitate to vent. "My family, Satvik. They want me to get married. Dimpu just called. He said Mom's worried about me being alone all the time. Everyone's expecting me to settle down, but I'm not sure if I'm ready."

Satvik looked at her thoughtfully, his expression a mix of understanding and support. "Charu, you've always followed your heart. You've done things your way, and you've achieved so much already. You can't let anyone dictate your choices now. This is your life, not theirs."

Charu nodded, appreciating Satvik's words. He had always been her motivator, reminding her of the importance of staying true to herself.

"I don't want to disappoint them, though. I feel like I'm failing them by not meeting their expectations." Charu admitted, her voice tinged with frustration.

Satvik reached across the table and placed a hand over hers. "You're not failing anyone, Charu. You're succeeding in ways they don't even understand yet. You're breaking barriers, paving a path for others to follow. You're a first-generation lawyer, and that's something to be proud of. You have to keep your focus on your dreams. Marriage and family will happen when the time is right, but you can't let anyone rush you into something you're not ready for."

Charu felt the weight lift slightly from her shoulders. Satvik's encouragement always had that effect on her, like a breath of fresh air after a long, suffocating day.

"But what if I never find balance? What if I lose myself in this fight for success and end up alone?" Charu asked, the fear of loneliness creeping into her voice.

"You won't lose yourself," Satvik said confidently. "You're already a strong, independent woman. And when the time comes for you to settle down, you'll know. Don't rush the process. Focus on being the best version of yourself first, and everything else will follow."

Charu smiled softly, feeling a sense of relief wash over her.

"Thanks, Satvik. I needed to hear that."

"Always here for you, Charu," Satvik said with a grin. "Now go out there and continue being the incredible lawyer you are. Your future is bigger than anything anyone can imagine."

The days that followed were filled with tension. Charu couldn't shake off the conversation with Dimpu, nor the growing sense of pressure from her family. She continued to focus on her work, but it became harder to ignore the nagging thought that she was neglecting her family's wishes.

Her parents, especially her mother, had always been her pillars of support. But with her career taking priority, Charu couldn't help but feel she was drifting away from them. Dimpu's call had been a reminder of the familial bond she had always cherished, and the guilt of potentially disappointing them weighed heavily on her heart.

As she sat in her office late one evening, Charu received another call—this time from her mother.

"Charu, when will you come home for a visit? Dimpu and I miss you. We haven't seen you in so long." Her mother's voice was gentle, but Charu could hear the longing in her words.

"I'll try to come soon, Mom," Charu replied, trying to sound reassuring. "I'm just really busy with some cases right now. But I'll plan a visit soon, I promise."

Hanging up the phone, Charu felt a sharp pang of homesickness. She had always felt caught between her two worlds—her family, who loved her unconditionally, and her career, which she had fought so hard to build.

She didn't want to lose herself in the struggle, but she also knew she couldn't give up the work that gave her life meaning. The question that lingered in her mind was: Could she find a way to balance both?

Chapter 12

Charu sat in her office, reviewing the new case that had landed on her desk that morning. It was unlike any case she had handled before—high-profile, highly sensitive, and deeply personal. A young man, Rajesh, had come forward as a whistleblower against a government agency accused of corruption. The evidence he had was explosive, and his courage to speak up was undeniable. However, his life was in grave danger. The people he was exposing were powerful, and they would stop at nothing to silence him.

"Charu, this case is more than just another legal battle," Satvik had said when they had discussed it over the phone earlier that week. "It's about justice—real justice—and you're the only one who can fight for Rajesh now. Don't back down."

Charu wasn't just fighting for Rajesh; she was fighting for the truth itself. But the weight of it all felt overwhelming. The stakes were so high, and the threats against Rajesh and his family were starting to escalate. Charu had spent nights researching, preparing, and strategizing, but there was a growing sense of fear that gnawed at her. This wasn't just a case about laws and loopholes—it was about life and death.

It was late evening when Charu received a call that shook her to her core. Rajesh's lawyer, a senior lawyer who had been working with Charu's firm on a collaborative basis, sounded panicked. "Charu, you need to get here right now. Rajesh... he's been kidnapped. The police have no leads, and we're losing time." Charu's heart pounded in her chest as she grabbed her coat and rushed out of the office. Her mind raced, flashing through every detail of the case, wondering if there was something she had missed, some sign that could have prevented this.

When she arrived at the law firm's headquarters, the team was already gathering. Satvik was there, standing near the entrance, looking grim.

"Charu, are you okay?" he asked, his voice low.

"I don't know, Satvik," she replied, her hands shaking. "I should have seen this coming. We've been pushing too hard for the truth, and now he's gone."

Satvik placed a steady hand on her shoulder. "You did everything you could, Charu. And you'll keep doing everything you can. We're not backing down."

Charu took a deep breath, trying to steady herself. She knew Satvik was right. She had no choice but to keep fighting, for Rajesh and for everyone who believed in the justice system.

The next few days were a blur of meetings with police, press conferences, and frantic attempts to locate Rajesh. Charu felt like she was being pulled in a million different directions. But even with the pressure mounting, one thing remained clear—her passion for the case. She refused to let fear dictate her actions.

"Charu, you've been at this for hours. Take a break," Satvik said, walking into her office with a cup of coffee.

Charu didn't even look up as she continued to go through case files. "I can't afford a break right now. The longer we wait, the more dangerous this gets. Rajesh is out there, and I have to find him."

Satvik stood by the desk, watching her. "I get it. But you're not superhuman, Charu. You need to take care of yourself too."

Charu finally looked up, her eyes tired but determined. "I'll rest when this is over. Right now, Rajesh's life is on the line. I can't stop until he's safe."

Satvik didn't argue. He knew Charu's resolve better than anyone. But he also knew the toll this case was taking on her, and he worried about what it was doing to her spirit.

Meanwhile, Dimpu had been following the news coverage of the case and had been texting Charu every day, trying to check on her well-being.

"Didi, please take care of yourself. You've been working non-stop for days. You don't have to do this alone."

Charu had responded briefly, "I'm fine, Dimpu. Just focusing on the case. Don't worry about me."

But Dimpu's words stuck with her, gnawing at her guilt. He was right. She didn't have to fight this battle alone. There were people who cared about her, who wanted to see her succeed, but also wanted to see her stay safe.

As Charu continued to fight for Rajesh, the pressure from her family, her friends, and the weight of the case started to make her question everything. Could she truly make a difference in a world that felt so corrupt? Could she be the advocate she had always dreamed of being, or was she losing herself in a system that didn't care?

Her thoughts were interrupted when a call came through—Rajesh had been found.

The relief Charu felt was immediate and overwhelming. She had won a small victory, but the fight was far from over. Rajesh was safe, but the forces behind his abduction weren't going to give up. Charu knew this was just the beginning of a long battle.

The next day, Charu sat with Rajesh in a private room at the hospital. His body was battered, but his spirit was unbroken.

"Thank you, Charu," Rajesh said softly, his voice hoarse. "I didn't think anyone would believe me. But you did. You never gave up."

Charu smiled, her heart swelling with pride. "I'm just doing my job. You're the one who showed true courage by speaking up. I'll make sure you get the justice you deserve."

As she left the hospital room, Charu felt a renewed sense of purpose. She was more than just a lawyer now. She was someone who could make a real impact on the world.

In the coming weeks, Charu faced the toughest battle of her career. She would fight not only for Rajesh's safety but also for the integrity of the legal system she had devoted her life to. She knew that the path ahead wouldn't be easy, but as long as she had the truth on her side, she was willing to face whatever came her way.

Her journey had only just begun.

<u>Chapter 13</u>

Charu had always been a fighter, but this case was unlike anything she had encountered before. With Rajesh safely recovered, Charu's next challenge was to ensure that the corrupt figures behind his abduction would be brought to justice. But as she stepped into the courtroom, the atmosphere was thick with tension. The opposition was fierce, their resources seemingly endless. They had the connections, the influence, and the power to make things difficult—perhaps even impossible—for Charu and her team.

Charu sat at the defense table, her mind racing as she listened to the arguments from the opposing side. They were using every trick in the book to discredit Rajesh, labeling him a liar and a criminal. But Charu knew better. She had the truth on her side, and that was something no amount of money or influence could take away.

"Your Honor," the opposing lawyer began, his tone condescending, "the defendant has no credibility. His allegations are nothing more than a desperate attempt to cover up his own criminal activities. There is no evidence to support his claims, and the defendant is simply trying to avoid facing the consequences of his own actions."

Charu clenched her fists under the table, her teeth gritting. She knew that these accusations were nothing but smoke and mirrors, but she couldn't let her emotions get the best of her. She had to stay calm, focused. She had to show the court—and herself—that she could handle whatever was thrown her way.

Satvik, sitting beside her, whispered just loud enough for Charu to hear, "Stay strong. We have the evidence. We just need to make them see it."

Charu nodded, taking a deep breath. She would need to be strategic. The truth had to come through, no matter how difficult it was to expose.

The courtroom grew quiet as Charu rose to present her argument. Her voice, although steady, carried the weight of everything she had worked for.

"Your Honor," Charu began, "I stand before you today not just as a lawyer, but as someone who believes in the fundamental principle of justice. We cannot allow those who hold power to manipulate the system and silence the truth. Rajesh is not a criminal. He is a hero—a whistleblower who risked everything to expose corruption that affects us all."

Charu's eyes locked onto the opposing lawyer as she continued, her words clear and precise. "We have irrefutable evidence, witnesses, and the truth on our side. The allegations against Rajesh are fabricated, designed to discredit him and protect those responsible for these heinous acts."

The room was silent as Charu presented the evidence, each document and witness statement supporting Rajesh's claims. The opposition tried to interrupt, but Charu stood firm, refusing to let them deter her. She knew that this battle wasn't just for Rajesh; it was for every person who had been wronged, for every whistleblower who had been silenced by fear.

As the trial continued, Charu felt the weight of the case pressing down on her. Every decision, every argument, could make or break the outcome. But she knew she couldn't afford to doubt herself. She had come too far, fought too hard. This case was not just about her—it was about the integrity of the legal system, about proving that justice could prevail against all odds.

One evening, after a particularly grueling day in court, Charu sat in her office, her head resting on her hands. Dimpu had called earlier, but she hadn't been able to pick up. Now, she stared at the phone, wondering how long she could keep pretending that everything was fine.

Just then, her phone rang again. It was Satvik.

"Charu, how are you holding up?" Satvik's voice was soft, filled with concern.

Charu let out a long sigh. "I don't know anymore, Satvik. I'm giving everything I have to this case, but the pressure is unbearable. Every time I think we're getting somewhere; they throw another obstacle in our way."

Satvik paused, then spoke with conviction. "I know it's tough, Charu, but you've come so far. Don't lose sight of why you're doing this. You're not just fighting for Rajesh. You're fighting for every person who has been silenced by fear. You're showing everyone that the law isn't just for the rich and powerful. It's for the people."

Charu smiled faintly, her spirits lifting just a little. "You always know how to put things into perspective, Satvik. Thank you. I just... I just don't know how much longer I can keep pushing like this."

"You're stronger than you think, Charu. And you're not alone. We're all in this with you."

Charu held the phone to her ear, feeling a warmth in her chest that she hadn't felt in days. "Thanks, Satvik. I really needed to hear that."

The following days brought even more challenges. The opposing side was relentless, throwing every legal maneuver they could think of to delay the proceedings. But Charu refused to back down. She knew that if she did, it would set a precedent that could harm countless others who sought justice.

The turning point came when Charu uncovered a hidden document—an email that linked the corrupt officials directly to the illegal activities. This was the evidence they had been waiting for. With the help of her team, Charu was able to expose the truth, revealing the full extent of the corruption and the lengths to which the perpetrators had gone to conceal it.

In court, when the final bombshell was dropped, the opposition had no choice but to concede. The truth had won.

As Charu walked out of the courtroom, her heart pounded in her chest. The case wasn't over, but this was the victory they had been fighting for. Rajesh was going to be safe, and the corrupt officials would finally face the consequences of their actions.

But Charu knew that the fight wasn't over. There would always be more battles to fight, more challenges to face. But for the first time in a long while, Charu felt something she hadn't felt before—hope.

Chapter 14

The courtroom was quiet as Charu stood in front of the judge; the weight of her previous victory still fresh in her mind. The case had turned in her favour, but she knew the battle was far from over. The corruption she had exposed ran deep, and the powerful individuals involved would not let it go without a fight.

Charu's phone buzzed on the table, breaking her concentration. It was a message from Satvik.

"Charu, we need to talk. The opposition has more influence than we thought. Be careful."

She read the message twice before slipping her phone back into her bag. The warning was not lost on her. Charu had always been aware that fighting against powerful individuals came with its risks, but she had never imagined how far they would go to silence her.

As Charu made her way out of the courthouse, she could feel eyes on her. The atmosphere had changed. It wasn't just about legal victories anymore—it was about survival. She had made enemies, and those enemies were not going to let her walk away unscathed.

Dimpu, her younger brother, was waiting for her outside. He was grinning, but Charu could see the worry in his eyes.

"Did you win?" Dimpu asked, his voice full of hope.

Charu nodded, but her expression was somber. "Yes, but the fight is far from over. We've won the battle, but they'll come after us harder now. I can feel it."

Dimpu's face tightened with concern. "I knew it. They'll try to intimidate you. You can't do this alone, Charu."

Charu smiled weakly, ruffling his hair. "I'm not alone, Dimpu. I have you, and I have Satvik. We'll get through this together."

Later that night, Charu sat in her office, her mind swirling with the implications of the case. The corruption she had uncovered was just the tip of the iceberg. The people involved had connections that reached deep into the political landscape, and they were not going to let their empire crumble without a fight.

Charu had just begun to make sense of everything when there was a knock on her door. She looked up to see Satvik standing in the doorway, his face serious.

"Charu, we need to talk."

She motioned for him to sit down. "What's going on? You're more serious than usual."

Satvik took a deep breath, glancing around the office before sitting down. "I've been getting some information. It's not good."

Charu leaned forward, her heart pounding in her chest. "What is it?"

"The people we're up against—they've got connections in the government. Powerful people who can make this whole thing go away with a single phone call."

Charu felt a chill run down her spine. She had suspected as much, but hearing Satvik confirm it made the reality all the more daunting.

"What do we do?" Charu asked, her voice barely a whisper.

Satvik looked her in the eye. "We fight back. But we need to be smart. They'll try to use the system against us. They'll attack you personally, professionally—anything to make you back down."

Charu's mind raced as she processed the information. "But I can't back down, Satvik. Not now. I've come too far. I can't let them win."

Satvik nodded, his expression softening. "I know. And I'm with you every step of the way. But we need to be prepared. We need to have a strategy. You're not just fighting for Rajesh anymore—you're fighting for everything you've worked for. Your career. Your reputation. Your future."

Charu took a deep breath, steadying herself. "We'll fight. And we'll win."

The days that followed were a whirlwind of strategy meetings, late-night research, and constant vigilance. Charu's every move was now under scrutiny, her every action watched. But she refused to be intimidated. She knew that if she could stay focused, she could turn the tide in her favour.

One evening, as Charu was leaving her office, she received an unexpected phone call. It was her sister, Neha.

"Charu, I've been hearing things," Neha said, her voice filled with concern. "Are you okay? You've been under a lot of pressure lately."

Charu smiled softly. "I'm fine, Neha. Just a little tired. But I'm okay."

Neha paused before speaking again. "Charu, you know I always wanted to be a lawyer, right?"

Charu blinked in surprise. "Of course. You've told me many times."

"Well, I never had the courage to follow through. The world of law—especially the world of first-generation lawyers—scared me. The struggles, the hurdles, the constant battles... I didn't think I could handle it. But seeing you, Charu... the way you've fought for everything you believe in... it's inspiring."

Charu's heart swelled with pride. "Neha, you've always been my inspiration. Don't you think you've got what it takes? If anyone can do it, it's you."

There was a pause on the other end of the line. "Maybe you're right, Charu. Maybe I can start again. Maybe... just maybe, I can fight my own battles like you did."

Charu smiled, her heart lifting. "You can, Neha. You've got the strength inside you. You just have to believe in it."

Later that week, Charu's fears were realized when she was summoned to a meeting with a powerful government official. The man was intimidating, his presence filling the room as he laid out his demands.

"Ms. Charu, you've done well for yourself, but you're treading in dangerous waters," the official said, his voice cold and firm. "If you drop the case now, I can make sure your career stays on track. I can ensure that you won't face any further challenges."

Charu stared at him, her heart racing. She had known this was coming. The temptation to back down was strong, but she wouldn't let fear dictate her future.

"I won't back down," Charu said firmly, her voice unwavering. "Not now, not ever."

The official smirked. "We'll see about that."

That night, Charu sat alone in her office, contemplating the path
ahead. She had come this far, and she wasn't about to give up now.
The political labyrinth she had stepped into was dangerous, but
Charu was more determined than ever to navigate it.
She had always fought for justice, for the truth. And no matter how
powerful her enemies were, she would keep fighting—for herself,
for her clients, and for the countless others who had been silenced
by fear.

Chapter 15

The phone calls and messages started flooding Charu's phone before she could even start her day. Satvik had sent an urgent text:

"Meet me at the office. We need to finalize our strategy."

Charu's mind raced. The official's threat was still fresh in her mind. She knew this was the beginning of something far more intense than any case she had handled before. But she was ready. Or at least, she told herself she was.

By the time Charu arrived at her office, Satvik was already there, pacing back and forth, his eyes sharp with concern.

"They're not backing down," Satvik said as soon as Charu entered. "They have too much at stake. You're not just dealing with one person anymore—you're up against an entire system."

Charu nodded, her face set with determination. "I know. But I've come this far, Satvik. I can't let fear stop me now. We have the truth on our side."

Satvik stopped pacing and looked at her, his gaze softening. "The truth is our weapon, Charu. But remember, it's not just about the law anymore. It's about strategy, influence, and power. We have to be ready for anything."

Charu took a deep breath, looking at the stack of papers on her desk. "I've been preparing for this my whole life. It's not just about me anymore, Satvik. It's about everyone who's ever been silenced by this system. I won't back down."

Satvik nodded slowly. "We'll fight together, Charu. You're not alone in this."

The next few days were a blur. Charu spent every waking moment strategizing, meeting with her team, and studying every legal loophole she could find. Her reputation was on the line, and so was everything she had fought for. The opposition, sensing her resolve, upped the ante—pressuring her with threats, phone calls, and even veiled attempts at bribery. But Charu stood firm, refusing to give in to their tactics.

One evening, as Charu sat at her desk, exhausted from the relentless pace, Dimpu knocked on her door, his face lined with worry.

"Didi, are you sure about this?" Dimpu asked, his voice soft, yet filled with concern. "I've seen how they've been pressuring you. This isn't just a legal fight anymore. It's dangerous."

Charu looked at him, her eyes tired but filled with determination. "I've always known that standing up for what's right comes with risks, Dimpu. But we can't live in fear. I have to do this—not just for me, but for people like Rajesh who can't fight for themselves."

Dimpu's eyes softened. "I know, Didi. I just want you to be safe."

Charu stood up and walked over to him, placing a hand on his shoulder. "I'll be fine. We'll be fine. Just trust me."

As the final showdown approached, Charu felt a surge of anxiety mixed with determination. She knew this case would make or break her career. She had no idea how deep the political corruption went, but she was about to find out.
The night before the crucial hearing, Satvik called Charu, his voice low and serious.
"Charu, I've been digging deeper. There's something big coming our way."
Charu's heart skipped a beat. "What do you mean?"
"I've learned that one of the judges on our case has ties to the opposition. It's not confirmed yet, but it's a serious conflict of interest. If we can expose it tomorrow, we might have a shot at taking them down."
Charu felt a wave of anger rise within her. "I knew they wouldn't play fair. But this is our chance, Satvik. If we can expose the truth, we can win. We can finally bring these people to justice."
Satvik's voice was firm. "We'll need to be careful. If they find out what we're planning, they won't hesitate to retaliate."
Charu took a deep breath, gathering her resolve. "We've come too far to turn back now."

The next day, Charu entered the courtroom with a calm exterior, though inside, her heart was racing. This was it—the moment that would define her career. She stood before the judge, her eyes scanning the room. The opposition's lawyers sat smugly, knowing they had the upper hand.

The judge, a man Charu had once admired for his fairness, looked down at her, his gaze betraying nothing. She could feel the weight of his unspoken allegiance.

Then, it was time.

"Your Honor, I have new evidence to present," Charu said, her voice steady. She held up a file with the incriminating documents Satvik had uncovered. "This document reveals that one of the judges presiding over this case has direct ties to the opposition. This is a clear conflict of interest, and I request that the judge recuse himself from this case immediately."

The courtroom went silent, and Charu could feel the tension rise. The judge's face remained neutral, but the opposition's lawyers immediately started protesting.

"This is an attempt to derail the case!" one of them shouted.

"I assure you, this is not an attempt to delay the proceedings. This is an attempt to ensure that justice is served without bias," Charu replied, her voice unwavering.

The judge looked down at the documents, his fingers lightly brushing over the pages. Charu's heart pounded in her chest. She

had just laid all her cards on the table. There was no turning back
now.

After what felt like an eternity, the judge stood up. "We will
adjourn for a brief recess while we review these allegations. Court
is adjourned."

In the hallway, Charu and Satvik stood side by side, their nerves on
edge. Charu's phone buzzed again—it was Dimpu.

"Didi, I know you're fighting hard. But remember, no matter what
happens, I'm proud of you."

Charu smiled, her heart swelling with pride. "Thank you, Dimpu.
You don't know how much that means to me."

Satvik glanced at her, his expression mixed with hope and concern.
"Do you think it'll work?"

Charu nodded, her voice steady despite the storm inside her. "It has
to."

The courtroom reconvened after the recess, and the judge made his
decision.

"After reviewing the allegations and the presented evidence, I have
decided to recuse myself from this case. A new judge will be
assigned immediately."

Charu's breath caught in her throat. This was a monumental victory. The opposition's plan to manipulate the system had been exposed, and now, they would have to face an impartial court. As she walked out of the courtroom, Charu's heart swelled with triumph. This was just the beginning of the battle, but it was a battle she was determined to win.

<u>Chapter 16</u>

The courtroom victory had given Charu a brief sense of triumph, but as the days passed, the battle was far from over. The opposition wasn't going to let go so easily. Charu knew that exposing the judge's conflict of interest had only scratched the surface of the web of corruption they were up against. But the news of the judge's recusal had already spread like wildfire, giving the public a glimpse of the truth. This was a battle now not just for the law, but for the people who believed in her.

Charu sat at her desk late one evening, the silence of her office only broken by the quiet hum of the fan. Dimpu had left for his studies, and Satvik was out gathering more evidence. She had become used to the solitude. It was her moment to think, to reflect, and to prepare for whatever came next.

Her phone buzzed.

It was a text from Satvik: *"We've got them. The opposition's network is more extensive than we thought. We need to act fast."*

Charu frowned, her fingers tapping nervously on the desk as she read the message. *"What do you mean? What did you find?"*

The response was quick: *"We found more evidence linking some high-profile politicians to the fraud. It's bigger than anything we expected. I'll meet you at the office in 30 minutes."*

Charu's heart raced. This was it—the moment she had been waiting for. But the reality of the situation started to set in. The opposition wasn't just a group of corrupt officials—they were powerful, dangerous people with the ability to destroy anyone who stood in their way.

At the office, Satvik had a stack of documents laid out on the desk, his face grim.

"Charu, they're not going to stop. We've hit a nerve, and now they know we're serious. They'll come after us."

Charu walked over to him, her mind racing. "I've been expecting this. It's not just about winning the case anymore—it's about surviving it. We can't let them scare us."

Satvik looked at her, his eyes softening. "You've changed, Charu. I remember when we started this journey. You were afraid, uncertain... But now, you're fearless."

Charu smiled faintly. "Fearless? I'm terrified, Satvik. But I've come too far to turn back now. I've fought for everything I've ever wanted, and I won't let these people destroy what I've worked for."

Satvik nodded, understanding her more than anyone. "Then let's make sure they know we're not backing down."

The days that followed were a blur of strategy meetings, long nights, and mounting pressure. The opposition began to use every dirty trick in the book to try to discredit Charu—public smear campaigns, bribing witnesses, and even threatening her family. But Charu stood tall, never once faltering in her belief that she was on the right side of this fight.

Dimpu, though young, had been a silent source of strength for Charu. Every time she felt overwhelmed, his innocent words reminded her of why she was doing this in the first place.

One evening, after a particularly grueling day at the office, Charu came home to find Dimpu sitting at the kitchen table, looking up at her with wide eyes.

"Didi, I don't understand all the stuff that's going on, but I know you're doing something important. You're fighting for everyone. For me, for everyone who's afraid to speak up."

Charu's heart swelled with pride. She walked over and ruffled his hair. "Thanks, Dimpu. That means everything to me."

As the case progressed, Charu's reputation began to spread beyond her small office. The media started to cover her story—her fight against the corruption that had plagued the legal system for years. People from all walks of life sent messages of support, and Charu's once-small practice began to gain clients who needed someone who would fight for justice, no matter the cost.

But with the attention came the pressure. Charu knew that the moment she stepped into the courtroom, all eyes would be on her.

This wasn't just a case—it was a war, one that would either make or break her career.

One evening, Satvik came to Charu with an idea that would change the course of the case.

"Charu, we need to bring the media into this. We've got the truth on our side, but they've been using their influence to sway public opinion. It's time we turn the tables."

Charu paused, considering the implications. "But that could backfire. If we go public, they might find a way to twist the narrative against us."

Satvik shook his head. "We're already in the fight of our lives. Hiding won't help. We need the truth to be heard, loud and clear. The people need to know what's at stake."

Charu thought for a moment, the weight of the decision settling over her. She had always fought in the shadows, quietly building her case, staying under the radar. But Satvik was right. If she wanted to bring about change, she couldn't afford to hide anymore. She had to stand up—not just for her clients, but for everyone who had ever been silenced by corruption.

"Okay, Satvik. Let's do it. We'll go public."

The next day, Charu held a press conference. The room was packed with journalists, cameras flashing as reporters shouted questions. Charu stood at the podium, her heart pounding, but her voice steady.

"I'm here today because I believe in justice. I believe in the law. And I believe that no one, no matter how powerful, should be above the law." Her words rang out, and the room fell silent as she continued. "What we are facing is not just a legal battle. It's a battle for the soul of our nation. And I'm not backing down."

The media erupted in a frenzy, and the story of her fight against the corrupt politicians and officials made headlines the next day. Charu was no longer just a small-town lawyer—she was a symbol of hope for the people who had been oppressed by the system.

The case was far from over, but Charu knew one thing: no matter how tough it got, she would never stop fighting for what was right. She had come a long way from the unsure, scared girl who once questioned her ability to succeed. Now, Charu knew her true strength—she was a warrior for justice, and nothing could stop her.

Chapter 17

The pressure of the case weighed heavily on Charu. It wasn't just about the legal battle anymore—it had become personal. Every day brought new threats, new obstacles, and new challenges. But Charu wasn't the same person she had been when she first started this journey. She had learned, grown, and adapted in ways she never thought possible. Now, it was all about survival, and the stakes were higher than ever.

One morning, as Charu walked into her office, she found an envelope waiting for her on her desk. It was unmarked, but the weight of it made her pause. As she opened it, a chill ran down her spine. Inside was a single note, written in bold, urgent letters:

"Stop. Or we will destroy everything you've worked for."

Charu's hand trembled slightly as she read the words. She had expected something like this, but it still stung. The fear wasn't new—it had become a constant companion since the day she'd taken on this case. But now, it was louder, more threatening.

That evening, Satvik arrived at the office with his usual determined look, though his eyes reflected the gravity of their situation.

"Charu, we've got to talk."

Charu looked up, already knowing what was coming. "I know. This is getting dangerous, isn't it?"

Satvik nodded; his jaw clenched. "We've been gathering more evidence. But I'm afraid we're pushing them into a corner. They're not just threatening you anymore—they're going after your family, Charu. Dimpu, your parents, everyone."

Charu's heart sank. She had always known that this fight would come with consequences, but hearing Satvik speak the truth made it feel more real, more immediate. She couldn't let them hurt her family. She had come so far, but was it worth risking everything for one case?

"What do we do now, Satvik?" Charu asked, her voice barely a whisper.

Satvik sighed. "We do what we've been doing all along—we fight. But we need to make sure we've got all our bases covered. We can't afford to take chances anymore. You have to be ready for whatever comes next."

Charu nodded, her resolve hardening. "I didn't come this far to back down now."

The next day, the opposition made their move. Charu's office was raided by authorities claiming that there were irregularities in her practice. Files were seized, and accusations were thrown at her left and right. It was a clear attempt to discredit her, to stall the progress of the case.

But Charu was undeterred. She had faced adversity before, and she wasn't about to let them destroy everything she had worked for.

Later that night, Charu sat at her desk, staring at the piles of documents before her. She couldn't afford to waste any more time. Every minute counted now. Her phone buzzed with a message from Dimpu.

"Didi, I'm scared. Please don't let them hurt you."

Her heart ached as she read his message. She had always wanted to protect him, to give him a future free of fear and struggle. But now, she couldn't shield him from the storm that was closing in on them. She picked up her phone and replied, her fingers shaking.

"Don't worry, Dimpu. I'll be okay. I promise you, I will fight until the end. For you. For all of us."

The words felt hollow, but she knew she had to say them. She couldn't afford to let him see her fear.

The next day, Satvik and Charu gathered their most crucial evidence—the proof that could bring the whole corrupt network down. They were running out of time, and the pressure was building. They had no choice but to take a risk.

They decided to go public once again, this time with their most damning piece of evidence. Charu had learned from her past mistakes. She had learned that silence would not win this fight.

The truth had to be heard, no matter what it cost her.

The media storm that followed was intense. Headlines screamed about the scandal, and Charu became the face of the battle against corruption in the legal system. The case had transcended personal victory—it was now a movement, and Charu was its leader.

Weeks passed, and the tension reached its peak. The case went to court, and the final showdown began. Charu stood in front of the judge, her nerves steady, her heart focused. This was the moment of truth. The opposition's lawyers were fierce, throwing every tactic they could to try to undermine Charu's case. But Charu had come prepared. She had spent sleepless nights going over every detail, ensuring she was ready for whatever they threw at her.

The judge, who had once been hesitant to allow such a high-profile case to proceed, now seemed to understand the magnitude of the situation. Charu knew she had won one battle already—the battle for justice in this courtroom.

But it wasn't just about the case anymore. It was about something deeper—something she had realized in the months of fighting, the countless hours of preparation and sacrifice.

Charu wasn't just fighting for a client or a case. She was fighting for every person who had ever been silenced, for every underdog who had been told they couldn't win. She was fighting for a future where the law truly protected everyone, no matter their background or their resources.

As the final arguments were presented, Charu stood tall. The opposition's arguments were crumbling under the weight of her evidence. The courtroom was silent as Charu delivered her closing statement.

"This case is not just about the law. It's about the integrity of the system. It's about the trust that every citizen places in our legal framework. If we allow the corrupt to flourish, if we allow them to walk free, then we betray everything this country stands for. But if we stand together, if we fight with everything we have, we can make a difference. I'm not just fighting for one case. I'm fighting for every person who has been wronged. For every person who has been forgotten. For everyone who believes in justice."

The words echoed in the courtroom, and Charu knew that her fight, no matter the outcome, had already changed everything.

Chapter 18

The days after the final arguments felt like a blur to Charu. She had poured everything into the case, and now, all she could do was wait. Every minute felt like an eternity as the courtroom buzzed with rumours, speculations, and whispers of the verdict that was yet to come.

It was a late afternoon when Charu's phone buzzed. She had been trying to focus on her work, but her mind kept drifting back to the trial. When she saw Satvik's name flashing on her screen, she quickly answered.

"Charu, it's over," Satvik's voice was calm, but Charu could hear the weight of his words. "The verdict is out. You need to be there." Charu's heart skipped a beat. She had known this moment would come, but now that it was here, it felt like the ground beneath her was shifting. "I'm on my way," she said, trying to steady her voice.

The courtroom was filled with a tense silence as Charu entered. She could feel the eyes of everyone on her—reporters, lawyers, clients, and strangers. The case had drawn so much attention that the room felt suffocating, as if the very air had been thickened with the pressure of what was about to happen.

The judge, an older man who had presided over the case with a no-nonsense attitude, rose from his seat. The room stood as a sign of respect. Charu's gaze locked on the judge as he began to speak. "After careful consideration of the evidence, the testimonies, and the arguments presented, this court has reached its verdict."

Charu held her breath, her hands clasped tightly in front of her. "In the case of Charu Gupta versus the defendants, I find in favour of the plaintiff. The defendants are guilty of corruption, fraud, and the abuse of power."

A wave of emotion flooded Charu's chest. She had done it. The impossible had been achieved. The corrupt were finally going to be held accountable. But before she could fully process the victory, the judge continued.

"However," the judge's voice grew heavier, "due to the complexities of the case and the individuals involved, the sentence will be decided at a later hearing. The nature of the crime warrants further deliberation regarding the appropriate penalty."

Charu's relief was short-lived. The victory felt bittersweet. While the corruption had been exposed, it would take more time and effort to ensure the criminals were properly punished. And Charu knew, deep down, that the battle was far from over.

Later that evening, Charu sat at her desk, staring at the file in front of her. The weight of the case was finally lifting, but new challenges were already beginning to take shape. The threats, the intimidation, the relentless pressure—it was all still there. She could feel the eyes of the system upon her, and she knew the fight would continue in ways she hadn't even anticipated.

Her phone rang again. This time, it was Dimpu.

"Didi, I heard the news. You did it! You won!" Dimpu's voice was full of excitement, and Charu could hear the pride in his words.

Charu smiled, despite the exhaustion that hung over her. "Yes, we did it. But there's still more to be done."

"I know," Dimpu said, his tone suddenly turning serious. "But Didi, I'm proud of you. You showed me what it means to fight for what's right. You're my hero."

Charu's heart swelled with love for her younger brother. The sacrifices she had made, the sleepless nights, the constant struggle—it had all been worth it for moments like this. "You're my hero too, Dimpu. And I'll keep fighting, not just for this case, but for all of us. We have to make sure this never happens again."

The next few weeks were a blur of media interviews, meetings with clients, and endless preparations for the next phase of the case. The pressure mounted as Charu continued to face the

consequences of her victory. But through it all, she remained
resolute.

Satvik was by her side every step of the way, offering advice,
encouragement, and even a few jokes to lighten the mood when the
weight of it all became too much.

"You know, Charu," Satvik said one evening as they sat in her
office, "you're making history. People will talk about this case for
years to come. You're changing the way the system works."

Charu looked at him, a tired smile tugging at the corners of her
lips. "I don't know about making history, Satvik. I'm just doing
what I had to do."

"No, you're doing more than that," Satvik replied, his eyes serious
now. "You're showing people that they don't have to accept the
way things are. You're proving that the system can be challenged,
that justice can be served, even when it feels impossible."

Charu took a deep breath. The weight of his words settled in her
heart. It was true. She hadn't just fought for this case. She had
fought for the idea that justice could still exist in a world that often
seemed so broken.

As the months passed, the case moved closer to its final stages.
Charu knew that the ultimate resolution was still out of her hands,
but she had already made peace with the outcome. She had done
everything she could. She had stood up when no one else would.

And now, no matter what happened, she would continue to fight—
for justice, for truth, and for the future of the legal system.

One evening, as Charu walked home after a long day at the office,
she paused to look at the stars above. The city was alive with
sound, but for a moment, everything felt still.
She thought of her sister, who had once dreamed of becoming a
lawyer but had been held back by fear. She thought of Dimpu, who
had looked up to her every step of the way. And she thought of
Satvik, who had always believed in her, even when she hadn't
believed in herself.
For the first time in years, Charu felt a sense of peace. She had
won more than just a legal battle. She had fought for the future, for
the idea that things could change. And no matter what lay ahead,
she knew one thing for sure—her fight was far from over.

Chapter 19

The days leading up to the final judgment felt like the longest of Charu's life. Every morning, she would wake up early, her mind already racing with what could go wrong. The burden of her first major case, the people depending on her, and the countless sleepless nights she had put in—all of it was now leading to this final moment.

The trial had been a landmark one, and Charu knew that the verdict would set a precedent. The weight of history hung on her shoulders, but she couldn't afford to think about that. The people who had trusted her, the ones who had been hurt by the system—those were the faces she focused on.

It was an unusually warm afternoon when Charu received the summons. The courtroom would convene in an hour. She stood by her office window, looking out at the busy streets, and exhaled deeply.

"This is it," she whispered to herself.

Dimpu had been messaging her throughout the day, keeping her grounded. His cheerful texts always made her smile, but today they felt like a lifeline. "You've got this, Didi. You've already won in my eyes. You've shown us all that no matter where we come from, we can make a difference."

Charu quickly typed back: "Thanks, Dimpu. I'm not sure what will happen today, but whatever it is, I'll keep fighting for all of us." With one last glance at her phone, she grabbed her files and headed out the door.

The courtroom was even more packed than usual. Media outlets were stationed in every corner, their cameras flashing. Charu felt her pulse quicken as she entered, her eyes instinctively seeking out Satvik. He was sitting in the front row, his eyes locked on her, offering a silent show of support. His presence gave her a strange calmness that steadied her nerves.

As Charu walked toward the witness stand, she felt a familiar sensation—the same one she had experienced many times before. This was no longer just about the law. It was about what she had stood for all along—the hope that justice could still be served. She wasn't just representing her client anymore. She was representing every first-generation lawyer who had ever felt like they didn't belong, every underdog who had ever fought against a broken system.

The judge entered, and the room fell silent.

"We are here today to deliver the final judgment in the case of Charu Gupta versus the defendants," the judge said, his voice firm and steady. "The court has weighed all the evidence, and after careful consideration, we are ready to pronounce our decision." Charu's hands were slightly trembling as she waited for the judge's words. But she remained composed, focusing on the greater purpose that had carried her this far.

"The court finds the defendants guilty of all charges, including corruption, fraud, and abuse of power," the judge continued. "In light of the severity of their crimes, and the damage they have caused to innocent lives, they will be sentenced to the maximum punishment allowed under the law."

A wave of emotion surged through Charu, but she kept her composure. This was what she had fought for. Justice. The law. Truth.

She looked to Satvik, and for the first time in months, the weight of the world seemed to lift from her shoulders.

The aftermath of the verdict was a whirlwind. Media outlets clamoured to interview her, reporters sought her out for sound bites, and every phone call she received seemed to come with more congratulations. But amid the praise, Charu felt oddly distant. The victory, while sweet, felt hollow in some ways. She had won, yes—but at what cost?

The cases didn't stop. The demands of her career continued to mount. But for a brief moment, Charu allowed herself to savor the sense of accomplishment.

She went back to her office that evening, her mind heavy with the thoughts of everything that lay ahead.

That night, Satvik came by her office to check on her. He knocked on her door before walking in, offering a smile that she hadn't seen in days. "You did it, Charu," he said, his voice full of admiration. "You showed everyone that the system can change, that one person really can make a difference."

Charu leaned back in her chair, feeling a quiet pride wash over her. "I didn't do it alone, Satvik. I had help. From you, from Dimpu, from everyone who believed in me when I wasn't sure if I believed in myself."

Satvik sat across from her, his eyes serious. "But you were the one who took the leap. You were the one who stood up and said, 'Enough.' That's the hardest part."

Charu smiled softly. "Maybe. But the hardest part is still to come. I can't rest now. This is just the beginning. There's so much more to be done, so many more people to help."

A week later, Charu was in her office, reviewing new cases when Dimpu called.

"Didi, I'm so proud of you. Everyone is talking about your victory. You've changed the way people think about the law."

Charu smiled as she leaned against her desk. "It wasn't just me, Dimpu. We all did it. We've just started making a change."

"I know. And I've been thinking... I want to be like you when I grow up. I want to fight for what's right, no matter how hard it is."

Her heart swelled with pride. "You already are, Dimpu. You've been fighting for your future every day, just like I fought for mine. Don't ever forget that."

Charu's journey had only just begun. The legal world was vast, and there were still battles to be fought. But as she looked around at her office, at the files stacked high on her desk, and at the people who had supported her—she knew one thing for certain.

She had made it. She had fought against the odds, and now, with her victory, she had set a path for others to follow. Charu Gupta was no longer just a first-generation lawyer; she was a symbol of hope for anyone willing to fight for justice.

And this was only the beginning.

<u>Chapter 20</u>

Charu had barely recovered from her first big victory when the next challenge came knocking at her door. It was not a case, not a client, but a situation she never expected—a challenge that threatened to unravel everything she had worked for.

It began when she received an email late one evening. The subject line caught her attention: "Re: Investigation into Charu Gupta and her Legal Practices". Charu's heart skipped a beat. She opened the email with a sense of dread, and what she read made her blood run cold.

The email detailed an anonymous complaint against Charu's legal practices, alleging misconduct, ethical violations, and even corruption. It was signed by someone claiming to be a whistleblower within the court system. The accusations were vague but potent enough to cast a shadow over everything Charu had worked for.

Her phone rang immediately after she finished reading the email. It was Satvik.

"Charu, have you seen it?" he asked, his voice urgent.

"Yes, Satvik. I don't know what to make of it."

"Don't worry. We'll handle this. This is just a distraction, a way to take you down. I know you. I know your integrity."

Charu's hand gripped the phone tighter. "But it's not just any distraction, Satvik. It's a well-timed one. They're targeting me now. What if there's truth to it? What if I've made a mistake?"

Satvik's voice softened. "Charu, I know you. You're not the kind of person who would ever compromise your values. We're going to investigate, and we're going to prove that this is just a baseless attack. Don't let them win."

Charu closed her eyes, taking a deep breath. "I'm scared, Satvik. What if this ruins everything?"

"It won't," Satvik reassured her. "Not if we fight back. You've been through too much to let something like this stop you."

Charu's thoughts began to race. She had worked so hard to get to where she was—fighting against every expectation, every doubt. And now, someone was trying to pull her down with shadows of doubt and rumors. But she refused to let that happen.

The next day, Charu decided to take action. She called in her most trusted colleagues—Satvik, her legal assistant, and a few other close friends from law school. They met in her office, and Charu explained the situation.

"We need to get to the bottom of this," Charu said, pacing in front of the whiteboard, her mind already working at full speed. "We'll start by tracing the source of this complaint. Someone is trying to ruin my career, and we have to find out who."

Satvik nodded. "Agreed. But we need to be careful. We don't want to escalate things by going on the offensive too soon. Let's gather evidence, cross-check the claims, and proceed with caution."

Charu's younger brother, Dimpu, had been listening quietly in the background. Finally, he spoke up. "Didi, don't worry. If anyone can clear their name, it's you. Just keep doing what you've always done—stay focused on the truth."

Charu smiled at him. "Thanks, Dimpu. That means a lot."

With a team in place, Charu set to work. Days turned into weeks as she dug through her past cases, reviewed all her interactions with clients, and spoke to her colleagues. Every detail was scrutinized. She poured over her professional relationships and the integrity of every case she had handled. It was exhausting, but Charu was determined. She couldn't afford to let this baseless claim define her career.

One afternoon, as Charu was reviewing a pile of legal documents, Satvik came to her office with a grim expression on his face.

"Charu, I found something." His tone was serious, his words measured.

Charu set down her pen. "What is it?"

"The complaint… it's connected to someone you represented years ago. A case that didn't go the way they expected. Someone from that case has been quietly pushing to discredit you. They've been planting rumors."

Charu frowned, trying to remember. "Which case?"

Satvik showed her the files. "A corporate fraud case. You were representing a small company that lost a significant amount of money because of a larger corporation's illegal activities. The client you defended didn't win, and it caused a huge backlash."

Charu's stomach sank. "That's the case where I was up against one of the wealthiest and most influential families in the city. They've got connections everywhere."

Satvik nodded. "Exactly. This complaint is their revenge. They've been quietly planting seeds of doubt about your integrity for years. Now it's come to light. But Charu, it's a smear campaign. We have the proof."

Charu stood up, her heart pounding in her chest. "So, what do we do now?"

Satvik placed a hand on her shoulder. "Now we take action. We go public. We expose them for what they really are."

Charu knew Satvik was right. This was her chance to prove her innocence once and for all. She spent the next few days preparing her defense, gathering all the evidence to counter the false claims.

She called on a few of her former colleagues who had worked on the corporate fraud case with her to vouch for her professionalism and integrity. One by one, she built the case against the people who had tried to destroy her.

The day of the hearing arrived, and Charu stood before the courtroom again, this time not just fighting for a case—but fighting for her very reputation. She had the evidence, she had the witnesses, and she had the truth on her side.
As the judge called the court to order, Charu's heart was steady. She knew this would be one of the toughest battles of her life, but she also knew she couldn't back down now.

The proceedings were long, tense, and filled with back-and-forth arguments. But in the end, Charu's team presented the undeniable proof of the smear campaign, and the false accusers were exposed for their corruption and greed. The judge ruled in Charu's favor, dismissing the allegations and reprimanding those who had tried to tarnish her name.

As Charu left the courtroom, Satvik was waiting for her outside. "You did it. I knew you would."

Charu nodded, a sense of relief washing over her. "It wasn't just me, Satvik. It was all of us—my team, my family. We proved that the truth always prevails."

Dimpu, who had been waiting nearby, ran up to her and hugged her tightly. "I told you, Didi. You're the strongest person I know. No one can take you down."

Charu smiled, looking around at the people who had supported her throughout this journey. "It's not about how hard you fall, Dimpu. It's about how many times you get back up."

And Charu Gupta, the first-generation lawyer, had just risen again—stronger than ever.

Chapter 21

After her victory in the courtroom, Charu's reputation soared to new heights. Clients flooded her office, eager to be represented by the woman who had stood tall in the face of a conspiracy. Yet, as her career blossomed, Charu found herself standing at a crossroads. The courtroom was no longer just a place for her to seek justice—it had become her second home, a place where she felt both powerful and vulnerable at the same time.

One evening, as she sat alone in her office reviewing files late into the night, she received a call from Satvik. His voice was familiar, a comforting presence in the whirlwind of her life.

"Charu, we need to talk." His tone was serious, pulling her out of her deep thoughts.

"What's going on, Satvik?" Charu asked, feeling a twinge of concern.

"You've been working nonstop. I can hear it in your voice. You need to take a break. You're burning yourself out."

Charu let out a sigh, rubbing her temples. "I can't, Satvik. There's too much at stake right now. My career… the cases. I don't have time to stop."

There was a pause on the other end of the line, then Satvik spoke softly. "Charu, I get it. You've fought so hard to get here. But you're not invincible. I've seen you lose sleep over clients who won't even remember your name in a few years. I've seen you push yourself so hard that you're running on empty. Is this the life you imagined?"

Charu's heart ached at his words. She leaned back in her chair, staring at the ceiling. "I don't know anymore, Satvik. I thought this was the dream. But lately… it feels like I'm losing touch with everything that mattered. The long hours, the constant pressure, the never-ending chase for justice—it's exhausting."

Satvik's voice softened. "Charu, you've worked so hard to get here, but don't lose yourself in the process. Take a step back, even if it's just for a little while. Find a balance. You can't pour from an empty cup."

Charu knew he was right. She'd been so focused on proving herself, on winning every case and silencing every doubt, that she had lost sight of the things that made her happy. She missed the simplicity of life before all of this—the days spent with her family, the quiet evenings with Dimpu, the laughter shared with Satvik during their late-night talks about the future. Somewhere along the way, she had forgotten what it meant to live, to breathe, and to simply *be*.

But just as she began to entertain the idea of taking a break, the phone rang again. It was her mother.

"Charu, Beta, I need to talk to you."

Charu's heart sank. "What's wrong, Ma?"

"It's Dimpu… He's not well. I'm worried about him."

Charu's stomach twisted. "What happened?"

Her mother explained that Dimpu had been feeling unwell for the past few days, but his condition was worsening. He had been avoiding his family's concern, claiming it was nothing serious, but his mother could tell something was off. Charu felt the weight of the situation hit her. Dimpu had always been her pillar of strength, and now, it was her turn to be there for him.

"Ma, I'll be there tomorrow. Don't worry, I'll take care of everything."

As the call ended, Charu sat in silence for a few moments, trying to process everything. Her mind was racing. She had just emerged from one battle, only to face another—this time, it was her family that needed her.

The next morning, Charu packed her bag and headed to Gaya. The train ride was long, but it gave her time to think. What had she been doing with her life? Was it worth it to keep chasing success at the cost of her health and happiness? The life she had built was admirable, but it felt hollow in moments like this—when her family, the people who had supported her from the very beginning, needed her the most.

When Charu arrived home, she rushed to Dimpu's room. He was lying on his bed, his face pale and his body weak. The sight of her younger brother so vulnerable broke her heart.

"Dimpu, what's going on?" Charu asked softly, sitting by his side.

Dimpu gave her a weak smile. "Didi, it's nothing. I'm just tired. Don't worry about me."

Charu shook her head. "Don't lie to me, Dimpu. I know you. You've been pushing yourself too hard. What's going on?"

Dimpu hesitated for a moment before speaking. "I've been stressed, Didi. With school, with everything going on… I guess I didn't realize how much it was affecting me."

Charu gently brushed his hair away from his forehead. "You don't have to do it alone, Dimpu. You can always talk to me."

Dimpu nodded, tears welling up in his eyes. "I don't want to disappoint you, Didi. You've always been the strong one. I feel like I'm letting you down."

Charu's heart ached at his words. She took his hand in hers. "Dimpu, you've never let me down. You're my family. You don't have to be strong all the time. I'm here for you, always."

That night, Charu sat in the quiet of her childhood home, reflecting on everything she had been through. She had worked so hard to prove herself, but in the process, she had neglected the people who mattered most. Her family had always been there for her, even when she couldn't be there for them.

She realized that the key to true success wasn't just in winning cases or gaining recognition—it was in maintaining the balance between personal and professional life. She couldn't afford to lose sight of what really mattered.

The next morning, Charu made a decision. She would take a step back from her overwhelming caseload. She would spend more time with Dimpu, support him as he navigated his own struggles, and find time for herself.

She knew the road ahead wouldn't be easy. The legal world was demanding, and success was never guaranteed. But one thing was certain—she wouldn't lose herself again in the process.

Chapter 22

Charu's decision to step back and focus on her family had given her a sense of peace she hadn't felt in years. She spent more time with Dimpu, helping him navigate his academic challenges and offering her support in every way possible. In the evenings, they would sit together, chatting about everything and nothing. Charu's life, once dominated by the weight of her career, now felt more balanced. She still worked hard, but her priorities had shifted—family, health, and self-care had become just as important as her work.

However, it wasn't long before the professional world called her back. One fateful afternoon, as Charu was wrapping up a case in her office, she received a call that would change everything.

"Charu, there's a case I need you to take on," her mentor, Mrs. Sharma, said on the other end of the line. "I know you're taking a break, but this case could make or break your career."

Charu paused, her mind racing. "What kind of case is it?"

"It's a high-profile case involving a powerful corporation. They're being accused of environmental violations, and the pressure to settle is immense. But if we win, it'll send a strong message. You've handled tough cases before, but this one will test you like never before. You're the best person for this."

Charu's heart began to race. She had been enjoying the balance she had created in her life, but the allure of such a case was hard to ignore. It was a chance to prove herself even further, to push her limits. But deep down, Charu knew that this case came with risks—risks that could pull her back into the relentless cycle of overwork and neglect that she had just escaped.

"I'll need some time to think about it," Charu said, her voice steady despite the whirlwind of thoughts in her head.

"Of course. But just remember, Charu, this could change everything for you."

Later that night, Charu sat on the balcony of her home, gazing at the stars. She needed to make a decision. Her phone buzzed, and she saw that it was a message from Satvik.

Satvik: *"I heard about the case. Don't let it overwhelm you, Charu. You've come so far. Don't forget why you started this journey in the first place."*

Charu smiled at his message, feeling the familiar warmth of his words. Satvik had always been a grounding presence in her life, offering her wisdom when she needed it most. She replied, "I'm torn, Satvik. This case could mean everything, but I don't want to lose myself again. I don't want to go back to that place where I'm consumed by work and forget about everything else."

Moments later, Satvik called her. "Charu, I understand what you're feeling. But you're not the same person you were when you started. You know your limits now. You know when to push and when to step back. This case could be the challenge you need, but you have to go into it with your eyes open."

Charu took a deep breath, considering his words. "You're right. I can't let it define me. I'll take the case, but this time, I'll do it on my terms. I'll set boundaries. And I won't lose myself in the process."

Satvik's voice softened, and Charu could almost hear the smile in his words. "I'm proud of you, Charu. You've learned so much. Just remember, you don't have to do this alone. You have people who care about you."

The next morning, Charu met with Mrs. Sharma to discuss the case further. The corporation involved was one of the largest in the country, and the stakes were high. The media was already covering the story, and the pressure to settle was mounting. Charu felt the weight of the responsibility on her shoulders, but she knew that this was the moment that could define her future.

As the meeting concluded, Charu walked out of the office, feeling the familiar rush of adrenaline that came with taking on a new challenge. But this time, she was determined to do things differently. She would handle the case with the same passion and dedication that had brought her success, but she would also be mindful of her limits.

For the first time in a long while, Charu felt a sense of balance between her professional ambition and personal well-being. She knew that the road ahead would be difficult, but she was ready for it. She wasn't just fighting for success—she was fighting for the life she had worked so hard to build.

Weeks passed, and Charu threw herself into the case. She met with experts, examined evidence, and worked tirelessly to build a strong case against the corporation. The media continued to cover the story, with the corporation using every resource at its disposal to discredit her efforts. But Charu stood firm, knowing that she had the truth on her side.

One evening, after a particularly grueling day in court, Charu returned home exhausted. Dimpu was sitting on the couch, waiting for her.

"How's the case going, Didi?" Dimpu asked, his eyes full of concern.

Charu collapsed onto the couch next to him. "It's tough, Dimpu. Every day is a new battle. But I can't stop now. I have to finish this. Too many people are counting on me."

Dimpu looked at her thoughtfully, then took her hand. "You've come so far, Didi. You've faced so much. Don't forget to take care of yourself too."

Charu smiled at her younger brother. "I'm trying, Dimpu. I promise, I'm trying."

But deep down, Charu knew that this case was the ultimate test. She couldn't afford to let her work consume her again. She had to find a way to win this case without losing herself in the process.

Chapter 23

The day of the final court hearing had arrived. Charu stood in front of the courthouse, her heart pounding in her chest. The atmosphere was thick with tension, the eyes of the media and the public watching closely. She had come so far, battling against one of the largest corporations in the country. The case had dragged on for weeks, testing her patience, her skills, and most of all, her resolve.

Now, it all came down to this—this final day.

Charu adjusted her glasses, straightened her blazer, and took a deep breath. She was no longer the uncertain young lawyer who had stepped into the courtroom years ago. She had grown, both professionally and personally. She had learned to balance ambition with self-care, to trust in her abilities without losing sight of what truly mattered.

"You've got this, Charu," she whispered to herself, taking another step forward.

Inside the courtroom, the atmosphere was electric. The defense team, representing the powerful corporation, was already seated at their table, looking confident and well-prepared. Charu's side was quieter, her small team of legal experts and assistants standing beside her. Mrs. Sharma, her mentor, gave her a reassuring nod from the back of the room.

As Charu approached her seat, Satvik's message flashed in her mind: "Don't forget, Charu. It's not just about winning—it's about standing your ground."

She took her place, adjusting the files in front of her. She wasn't just representing herself today—she was representing every person who had ever been silenced by power and greed. She was fighting for justice, not just for her client, but for everyone who had been wronged.

The judge entered the courtroom, and the proceedings began.

"Counselor Charu, you may proceed," the judge said, his voice stern and commanding.

Charu stood up, her legs steady, her hands slightly trembling as she adjusted her notes. But the moment she opened her mouth, all traces of fear vanished.

"Your Honor," Charu began, her voice firm, "the evidence we have presented clearly shows that the corporation violated environmental laws, causing irreversible damage to our ecosystem and the communities that depend on it. Despite their attempts to discredit us, we have proven, beyond a reasonable doubt, that their negligence led to the devastation we see today. It is time for them to be held accountable."

The defense lawyer, a sharp-dressed man with a smug expression, immediately stood up. "Your Honor, the evidence presented by the plaintiff is circumstantial at best. We deny all accusations of wrongdoing and urge the court to dismiss the charges."

Charu's eyes narrowed as she looked at the defense team. She knew their tactics—they would do everything in their power to manipulate the court and distract from the truth. But she wasn't intimidated. She had faced much worse, and she was not going to back down now.

"Your Honor," Charu said, standing tall, "the defense may try to cloud the issue with technicalities, but the truth is clear. The corporation's actions have caused irreparable harm. The people who live in the affected areas have been robbed of their land, their health, and their futures. This case is not just about business—it's about people's lives."

As she spoke, Charu could feel the weight of her words in the room. The silence was deafening, the judge's eyes fixed on her as she continued.

"We must send a message that no one is above the law, no matter how powerful they may be. If we let them go unpunished, we send the message that corporate greed can override the rights of individuals and communities. I ask this court to do what is right, not just what is easy."

Charu sat down, her heart racing. She had given everything she had to that moment. Now, it was in the hands of the judge.

The courtroom remained still, and for what felt like an eternity, no one spoke. Finally, the judge leaned forward, his expression unreadable.

"The court will recess for the day. We will reconvene tomorrow for closing arguments."

That evening, Charu walked out of the courthouse, her head spinning. She had delivered her best argument, but the pressure weighed heavily on her. The media had been relentless, and the corporation's legal team had spared no effort in attacking her character and her case. She felt exhausted—physically, emotionally, and mentally.

Dimpu, sensing his sister's fatigue, was waiting for her when she returned home. He handed her a cup of tea without saying a word.

Charu smiled at him, grateful for his presence.

"You did great today, Didi," Dimpu said softly.

Charu sighed, sinking into the couch beside him. "I'm not sure, Dimpu. This case is so big. It feels like everything is on the line."

"But you've already come so far," he replied, his voice full of conviction. "You've already won by getting this far. No one thought you could, but you've proven them all wrong. You're stronger than you think."

Charu looked at her brother, her heart swelling with pride. She had worked hard to provide him with a better life, but in moments like this, it was clear that Dimpu had also given her strength.

The next day, Charu stood before the judge once again, ready to deliver her closing argument. The defense team had gone first, attempting to poke holes in her case, but Charu remained calm, determined to stay focused.

"Your Honor," she began, "I stand before you today not just as a lawyer, but as a woman who believes in justice. I've fought hard to get here, and I've seen firsthand the damage that unchecked corporate greed can do to communities and the environment. But this case isn't just about winning—it's about doing what's right." She could feel her words resonate, the weight of the courtroom's silence speaking louder than anything else. "Justice is not always easy. It doesn't always come in the form we expect. But it's what keeps us moving forward, what keeps us from giving up. I trust this court will make the right decision, not just for my client, but for every person whose voice has been silenced."

Charu sat down, her heart in her throat as she waited for the judge's verdict. The courtroom seemed to stretch out, every second feeling like an eternity.

Finally, the judge spoke.

"After careful consideration of the evidence presented, this court finds in favour of the plaintiff."

A wave of relief swept over Charu. She had done it. She had won.

Chapter 24

Charu's victory in court sent waves through the legal community. Her name was now synonymous with perseverance, and she was regarded as a rising star in the field of law. Headlines praised her strategy, her ability to stand firm in the face of adversity, and her ability to bring down a corporate giant. But as the accolades poured in, Charu found herself grappling with a new dilemma.

Her life had always been about fighting for justice, for the underdog, for what was right. But now, as she sat in the quiet of her office, surrounded by congratulatory messages and newspaper clippings, she wondered if this victory had brought her what she truly needed. Was this what success really felt like?

Dimpu had been overjoyed by her win. He had become her biggest cheerleader, frequently boasting about his sister's accomplishments to anyone who would listen. But Charu couldn't help feeling a sense of emptiness that she couldn't explain. She had fought so hard for this moment, but in the quiet aftermath, something felt missing.

"Didi, you're a hero now! I told you you'd do it," Dimpu said, his face glowing with pride.

Charu smiled, but her eyes didn't match the joy in her brother's voice. "Thanks, Dimpu," she said softly, before quickly changing the topic. "I'm just glad it's over."

Satvik, who had been her steady support throughout the case, noticed her unspoken unease. He called her that evening to check in, knowing she had been through a whirlwind.

"Charu, I'm proud of you. You proved everyone wrong. You won. But how do you feel?" Satvik asked, his voice kind but probing.

Charu sighed and sank into the chair. "Honestly, Satvik... I feel a little lost. I thought this victory would feel like a dream come true, but instead, I feel... disconnected. Like I've been chasing something my whole life, and now that I've caught it, I'm not sure what to do with it."

Satvik paused before responding. "You're not alone in feeling that way. We all think that success will come with a sense of completion, but the truth is, it's not the destination—it's the journey that defines us. It's easy to get caught up in the idea of winning, but real success comes from the impact you make, the difference you bring to the world, and the way you stay true to your purpose."

Charu listened intently, the weight of his words settling into her heart. "But what about the fear that if I don't keep pushing, I'll fall behind? What if everything I've worked for falls apart?"

"You've already proven that you can handle whatever life throws at you, Charu," Satvik said. "You're not defined by the cases you win or lose. You're defined by your ability to keep going, to stay true to your values, and to find balance in everything you do. Don't let your fear of the unknown dictate your future."

Charu took a deep breath. Satvik was right. She had spent so many years chasing validation through her work, through the recognition and the victories. But now, she needed to start defining success on her own terms—success that was not tied to the number of wins, but to the way she lived her life.

Weeks passed, and Charu found herself reflecting more on the things that truly mattered. She had been so focused on her career, on proving herself, that she had neglected the simple joys of life. She started spending more time with her family, especially Dimpu. She took time off from work to visit her mother in Gaya, a trip that reconnected her with her roots and helped her reconnect with the core values that had driven her in the first place.

One evening, as she sat with Dimpu in their childhood home, the house filled with the scent of fresh chai, she finally found the courage to speak her mind.

"Dimpu, I've realized something recently. Winning this case, earning recognition—it's all important, but it's not everything. I've been so caught up in proving myself to the world that I forgot why I started this journey in the first place."

Dimpu looked at her, his eyes full of curiosity. "What do you mean, Didi?"

Charu smiled softly, looking out the window at the stars. "I started this because I wanted to help people, to fight for the ones who didn't have a voice. But along the way, I got lost in the idea of success, in the pressure to always be the best, to always be winning. Now, I realize that it's okay to step back, to find balance."

Dimpu nodded, understanding his sister more than she realized. "I think you've always known that, Didi. You've always helped people, even when no one was looking. This win—it's just one chapter. There's so much more you can do."

Charu took a deep breath, her heart lighter than it had been in weeks. She had spent so many years worried about the future, about what people thought of her, about proving her worth. But now, for the first time, she felt free. Free to follow her own path, free to redefine success for herself.

The next day, Charu returned to her office with a renewed sense of purpose. She didn't need to chase the spotlight anymore; she needed to focus on the cases that mattered most, the people who truly needed her. She met with her clients, offering them the same care and attention that had always been the hallmark of her practice. She worked on pro bono cases, helping the marginalized and the unheard, rediscovering the joy she had once felt when she first became a lawyer.

In the quiet moments, Charu found herself reflecting on her journey—the struggles, the sacrifices, the victories, and the failures. Each step had shaped her, but it was the journey itself that had given her the most.

Her victory in court was just the beginning. The true success, Charu realized, was in the difference she made. It wasn't about the title or the recognition—it was about staying true to who she was and using her skills to build a better world, one case at a time.

Chapter 25

Charu's life had always been a whirlwind of work, deadlines, and the never-ending chase for justice. But after that realization, something had shifted within her. It wasn't just about being the best anymore—it was about being the best version of herself, about making a meaningful impact and finding joy in the small moments that had once seemed insignificant.

She started incorporating balance into her life. She spent more time at home with Dimpu, reminiscing about their childhood days and sharing stories from her legal battles. They would sit for hours, sipping chai, laughing over old memories, and discussing her future. Dimpu, now a teenager, was becoming a young man with aspirations of his own. He had started to admire his sister not only for her legal prowess but also for the way she had learned to juggle her career with the needs of her family.

One evening, as Charu was at the dinner table, Dimpu leaned over to her, his tone serious. "Didi, do you ever think about what happens next? Like, what will you do after you've done all the big cases?"

Charu smiled, placing her fork down. "What do you mean by 'what happens next?'"

Dimpu shrugged. "I don't know... I mean, you've done everything you could have ever dreamed of. You've won big cases, proved yourself in front of everyone. But what if you've reached the top? What happens when there's no higher place to go?"

Charu thought for a moment before answering, her eyes thoughtful. "Dimpu, there's always more to do. It's not about reaching the top. It's about the people you help along the way. The difference you make in someone's life—sometimes that's the real victory."

Dimpu nodded, though he still didn't entirely understand. But he trusted her wisdom.

Satvik, who had continued to be Charu's rock throughout her journey, noticed the change in her too. He could see that the pressure that had once weighed her down had started to lift. Charu was not only handling her career with grace, but she was also making time for herself. She began traveling for short breaks—visiting old friends, going on weekend hikes, and attending social events that didn't have anything to do with work.

One evening, they met at their favorite café. Charu, sipping her coffee, looked at Satvik across the table and asked, "Do you ever feel like we spend so much of our lives chasing something, only to realize that it was never the thing we were supposed to be chasing?"

Satvik, ever the philosopher, thought for a moment before replying. "I think we all do. We chase success, recognition, approval from others. But in the end, we realize that it's the relationships we build and the integrity with which we live that matter the most. You've always had that, Charu. You just needed to see it."

Charu smiled. "I know now. It's not about proving myself anymore. It's about finding peace in what I do and how I live. Maybe the most important case I've ever won is the one where I learned to stop trying to impress others and simply be myself." Satvik raised his cup in a silent toast. "Here's to finding yourself, Charu."

As Charu continued to reshape her life, her professional success didn't slow down. In fact, her reputation grew even stronger, but now it was built on a foundation of balance and authenticity. Her clients appreciated her not just for her legal expertise, but for the compassion she showed in every case she took on. She worked tirelessly on pro bono cases, advocating for people who had nowhere else to turn, and she started to focus on cases that mattered deeply to her.

One such case involved a group of women who had been unfairly treated by a corporate giant in a small town. The case was difficult, and many thoughts it wouldn't win, but Charu fought for them with everything she had. It wasn't about the money or the fame—it was about justice. And when she won, it wasn't just a victory for those women. It was a reminder to Charu that the real purpose of her work was to fight for those who couldn't fight for themselves.

Months later, Charu found herself reflecting once again, this time in her office. She had just finished a meeting with a new client who had been wrongly accused of a crime he didn't commit. As she prepared her arguments, she couldn't help but think about how far she had come from the girl who had been terrified of walking into that first courtroom. She had faced rejection, doubt, and endless struggles, but it had all led to this moment.

Dimpu knocked on her office door, his face lighting up as he stepped in. "Didi, I got into college! I'm going to study law!" he announced, his voice filled with excitement.

Charu couldn't help but feel a surge of pride. "I'm so proud of you, Dimpu! You've got a long road ahead of you, but I know you can do it."

He grinned. "I've learned from the best, haven't I?"

Charu laughed, feeling a warmth in her heart. "You've always been the best, Dimpu. Now you just have to believe in yourself as much as I believe in you."

She realized, in that moment, that her journey wasn't just about her own success—it was about passing on what she had learned to those who came after her. It was about showing them that the fight, no matter how difficult, was worth it. And that sometimes, the hardest battles weren't the ones fought in courtrooms—they were the ones fought within ourselves.

<u>Chapter 26</u>

It had been a few months since Dimpu started his law studies, and Charu was proud to see him embrace the profession she had once felt so alone in. The quiet moments at home were becoming more frequent, and with them came the realization that she was content. She had everything she had worked so hard for—success, respect, and love from her family and friends.

But that serenity was about to be tested.

One afternoon, while Charu was working on a case involving a corporate fraud scheme that had hurt hundreds of small business owners, she received a call from an old colleague, Sameer. His voice on the other end was shaky.

"Charu… I need your help. It's about one of the cases we worked on a few years ago—the one involving the construction company and those land disputes."

Charu's brow furrowed. That case had been messy, with a lot of political connections and shady dealings. She had fought tirelessly for the landowners, but the case had ultimately been swept under the rug. "What's going on, Sameer?"

"The truth is coming out. Some of the documents we thought were destroyed are surfacing again. I think it's all part of a bigger conspiracy. Charu, the people we fought against—they've been hiding so much. They're willing to do anything to silence the truth."

Charu's pulse quickened. She had heard the rumours—there were whispers about deep corruption within the system, but she had never imagined her past cases would bring her face-to-face with it.

"Are you saying they're going after you?" she asked.

"They're going after everyone who was involved. And that includes you."

Her thoughts spun. She couldn't believe it. The system—the very one she had spent her entire career fighting to uphold—was now turning against her. It was one thing to face personal battles and challenges in the courtroom, but this felt like a betrayal of everything she had believed in.

"Where are you now?" Charu asked, her tone sharp.

"I'm laying low for now. But I need your help. This is bigger than we thought. We have to expose it—before it's too late."

Charu hung up, her mind racing. She knew the risks. The legal world wasn't kind to whistleblowers, and exposing corruption of this scale could ruin her career. But she also knew that turning a blind eye wasn't an option. She had spent her entire career fighting for justice, and now, it was time to fight for her own.

The next day, she called Satvik, who had become not only her friend but a sounding board through her toughest decisions.

"Satvik, we need to talk," Charu said, her voice tense.

Satvik, sensing her urgency, agreed to meet her in their usual café.
When Charu sat down across from him, she wasted no time.
"It's bigger than we thought. There's a conspiracy surrounding the land dispute case we worked on. I'm being targeted now, Satvik. If I go after this, they'll come for me. They'll try to destroy my career, my reputation, everything I've worked for."

Satvik leaned back, his gaze steady. "You know what this means, don't you? If you go after them, you could lose everything. But if you don't, you'll never be able to live with yourself. They've built an empire on lies, and if you have the power to bring it down, then it's your responsibility."

Charu's fingers drummed nervously on the table. "I know… I know. But I'm scared. Scared of losing everything I've worked for. I've fought so hard to get here, Satvik. And what if it's all for nothing? What if I end up just another casualty in this broken system?"

Satvik placed his hand over hers, his voice calm but firm. "Charu, the system is broken, that's true. But you've always been the one who believed in making it right. If anyone can fight this, it's you. You've shown the world time and again that no matter the odds, you stand for what's right. Don't let them take that away from you."

Charu looked at him, her heart swelling with gratitude for his unwavering support. "I don't know what I would do without you, Satvik. You've been there through all of this."

Satvik smiled, a small but knowing smile. "You've got this, Charu. You've already fought battles no one else had the courage to fight. This one is just the next step."

In the following weeks, Charu's world became a whirlwind of preparations. She dug through old files, contacted whistleblowers, and reached out to journalists who could help expose the truth. As the pieces of the puzzle came together, it became clear that this wasn't just a legal case—it was a battle for the very integrity of the system that had defined her career.

But the deeper Charu dug, the more dangerous it became. Threats started arriving—anonymous phone calls, veiled warnings. Her phone was hacked, and her movements were being tracked. Charu realized that these people would stop at nothing to protect their empire. She couldn't let fear stop her, though. Her mission was greater than her own safety.

One night, as she was sifting through documents in her office, she heard a knock at the door. It was Dimpu, his face pale with worry.

"Didi, I don't want you to go down this path. It's dangerous. They're going to hurt you. I don't want to lose you like we lost Mom. Please, think about it."

Charu pulled him into a tight hug, her heart breaking for the fear in his voice. "Dimpu, I promise you, I'm doing this because I have to. I have to fight for justice, not just for us, but for everyone who can't fight for themselves. This is who I am. This is what I do."

Dimpu pulled away, his eyes filled with uncertainty, but he nodded. "I know, Didi. Just promise me that you'll be careful."

Charu nodded, though she knew that the road ahead would be anything but easy.

Chapter 27

Charu's fight had entered a dangerous new phase. The walls around her seemed to be closing in as she uncovered more about the conspiracy that threatened to undo everything she had worked for. Each step forward felt like stepping deeper into a web of deceit, with powerful forces working tirelessly to ensure the truth remained buried.

After weeks of sifting through documents and interviewing witnesses, Charu had discovered something that shook her to the core. The construction company that had been involved in the land dispute wasn't just engaged in illegal land acquisitions—it was linked to several high-ranking political figures and major corporations. These figures had their hands in everything from environmental violations to money laundering. They were untouchable, and now, Charu had become their target.

Her phone buzzed in the middle of the night. It was Sameer.

"Charu, they know. They're coming for you. You need to stop digging—"

Before he could finish, the call dropped. Charu stared at the screen, her heart pounding. She quickly re-dialled his number, but it went straight to voicemail. Panic surged through her, but she quickly pushed it aside. She couldn't afford to be scared now. She needed to act, and fast.

The next morning, Charu called Satvik, her voice steady despite the fear creeping into her thoughts. "Satvik, I need your help. It's getting worse. Sameer called me last night... He said they know I'm investigating, and I don't know if he's safe anymore."

Satvik didn't hesitate. "I'm on my way. We'll figure this out together. But Charu, you've been through too much already. You can't back down now. Not after everything."

Charu nodded, trying to steady her breath. She had always been strong, but the weight of the situation was suffocating. She had built her career on the belief that justice was within reach, but now it felt like she was chasing a dream that was slipping further away.

That evening, as Charu and Satvik met in a dimly lit café, Satvik's expression was serious. "We need to make sure this gets to the right people. If we go public with this, the backlash could be enormous, but if we don't, they'll silence you, Sameer, and everyone involved. We can't let them get away with it."

Charu exhaled deeply, staring at the pile of documents she had gathered. "I know, Satvik. But the risks... If I do this, it could ruin my career. It could ruin everything. I could lose my law license, my reputation, everything. The system is broken. It's so corrupt. I can't fight this alone."

Satvik reached across the table, placing his hand over hers.
"You're not alone, Charu. You have me. You have Dimpu. You have the truth on your side. And you've got the courage to stand up when no one else will. I know it's scary, but you've already overcome so much. You're not about to back down now."
Charu's eyes filled with gratitude, but her voice trembled slightly as she replied, "But what if it's all for nothing? What if I fight for justice, and in the end, they still win? I'm just one person against a system that's been in place for years. How do I take them down?"
Satvik leaned back, his gaze unwavering. "One step at a time. We'll start by exposing the evidence. We can't let them bury it. We'll reach out to the press, to the public. The more people who know, the harder it will be for them to silence you. But we have to act now. We can't afford to wait."

With Satvik's help, Charu began preparing a detailed exposé of the conspiracy. They contacted journalists, shared the evidence, and began to strategize how they would present the story to the public. But just as things were falling into place, Charu received another call—this one from Dimpu.

"Didi... I'm scared. I don't want you to go through this. It's too dangerous."

Charu's heart ached as she heard the fear in her younger brother's voice. "Dimpu, listen to me. This is the hardest thing I've ever

done, but I can't back down now. I promised myself that I would stand up for what's right, no matter the cost. I'm doing this for you, for everyone who's been silenced by people like this. Please understand."

"But what if you lose? What if they hurt you?"

Charu took a deep breath. "I won't lose, Dimpu. Not if I have anything to say about it. I've come too far to let fear control me. This fight... it's bigger than just me. It's about making sure people like us—people who have never had a voice—finally get one."

As Charu and Satvik continued to dig deeper into the corruption, they began to uncover more startling truths. The conspiracy ran deeper than anyone could have imagined, involving not just the politicians and business tycoons but also several high-ranking officials within the legal system itself. It was as though the very foundation of the law had been built on lies.

One evening, Satvik received a call from an anonymous source.

"You're getting too close, Satvik. You need to stop. There's still time to walk away."

Satvik didn't flinch. "You think you can scare me into silence? I'm not afraid of you."

The voice on the other end laughed, cold and menacing. "You should be."

The line went dead, leaving a sense of foreboding hanging in the air. Charu's heart skipped a beat. They were being watched. The threat was real. And yet, she knew she couldn't back down now. If she did, everything she had worked for would have been in vain.

The day they finally went public with the evidence, Charu's world changed. Media outlets picked up the story, and public outrage spread like wildfire. The powerful figures involved in the scandal tried to discredit Charu, but the truth had already taken root. People began to rally behind her, offering their support, even as the threats grew more frequent.

As the weeks passed, the case gained momentum, but so did the backlash. Charu was pulled in multiple directions—handling her practice, managing the growing media circus, and preparing for what could be a lengthy and dangerous legal battle. But every step, every challenge only strengthened her resolve. She had made it this far, and she wasn't about to back down.

One afternoon, as she sat in her office, reviewing the evidence one last time, Dimpu walked in, holding a letter in his hands. His expression was grave.

"Didi, they've taken Sameer. He's gone. They..." Dimpu choked up, his voice trembling.

Charu stood up, her blood running cold. "No… No, they can't do this. Sameer was helping me. We can't let them win, Dimpu." She turned to Satvik, her eyes blazing with determination. "This is it. We can't stop now. Sameer's disappearance just made it personal."

<u>Chapter 28</u>

The world around Charu was no longer the same. What started as a legal battle for justice had turned into a personal war—one where the stakes were higher than ever before. Sameer, the friend who had stood by her side, was gone, taken by the very people who had tried to destroy everything she stood for. But Charu wasn't going to let them win. She had come too far, and the truth was finally in her grasp.

Despite the mounting pressure, Charu remained resolute. The courtroom was her battlefield, and she had learned to fight with every ounce of strength in her. Every obstacle she faced, every setback, made her more determined. There was no turning back now.

Charu spent long nights preparing her case, pouring over evidence, strategizing with Satvik, and preparing for the inevitable confrontation in court. She had become more than just a first-generation lawyer; she had become a symbol of resilience for everyone who had ever been silenced by a corrupt system. Charu knew this was her moment, and she would fight to the very end.

The day of the trial arrived. Charu walked into the courtroom with the weight of the world on her shoulders, but her head held high. Her heart pounded, but she was no longer afraid. She had faced countless challenges, and each one had taught her something invaluable. Today was no different. The courtroom was filled with people—the press, lawyers, and members of the public who had followed the case. They were all watching her.

Charu stood at the podium, facing the judge, her voice steady as she presented the case. The evidence was overwhelming, the truth undeniable. She could feel the eyes of the powerful figures in the room—the politicians, the businessmen, the corrupt officials—squirming as she slowly dismantled their lies.

For hours, Charu argued with precision and clarity. She showed the world the lengths to which these powerful people had gone to exploit and deceive. She laid bare the corruption that had been hidden for so long. With every argument she presented, every piece of evidence, Charu felt stronger. This was her time to make a difference, to prove that the system could still work for the common man.

In the final moments of the trial, Charu stood before the judge, her voice unwavering. "I am not just a lawyer. I am the voice of those who cannot speak for themselves. The people whose lives have been ruined by the greed and corruption of those who believe they are untouchable. I am here today, not just to win a case, but to ensure that justice is served—because justice matters. And the truth is worth fighting for, no matter the cost."

The courtroom fell silent, the weight of her words sinking in. The judge took a long pause before delivering his verdict. "The court finds the accused guilty of all charges. They will be held accountable for their actions. This case serves as a reminder that no one, regardless of their power or influence, is above the law." Charu exhaled, her heart swelling with pride. She had done it. The corrupt system had been brought to its knees. But more importantly, she had done it as a first-generation lawyer—someone who had started with nothing and fought her way to the top.

The months that followed were a whirlwind. The case became a landmark, a symbol of what one determined individual could achieve against overwhelming odds. Charu's reputation grew, and she became an inspiration to countless others, especially first-generation lawyers like herself.
But Charu knew that the victory was just the beginning. She had made a difference, but the fight for justice was far from over. There were still many battles to be fought, many wrongs to be righted.
And Charu was ready.

One evening, as Charu sat in her office, reflecting on everything she had accomplished, Dimpu walked in, holding a newspaper in his hands. "Didi, look at this. You're on the front page!"

Charu smiled, but it wasn't the fame or recognition that mattered to her. It was the lives she had touched, the people who had come forward, inspired by her courage to fight for what was right. "I couldn't have done it without you, Dimpu. Without Satvik. Without all the people who believed in me. This victory is ours."
Dimpu grinned, proud of his sister. "You've shown us all that anything is possible. You proved that being a first-generation lawyer doesn't mean you're destined to fail. You've taught me, and so many others, that if you believe in something, and work hard enough for it, nothing can stand in your way."
Charu's eyes glistened with emotion. She had sacrificed so much to get to this point. She had faced fear, doubt, and opposition from all sides. But in the end, it was her persistence, her unwavering belief in justice, that had led her to victory.

That night, Charu lay in bed, staring at the ceiling. Her mind raced as memories of her journey flashed before her eyes—her struggles, her sacrifices, the doubts that had haunted her, and the people who had helped her along the way. She had fought not just for herself, but for all those who had ever felt powerless in the face of injustice.
Her phone buzzed, and she picked it up to see a message from Satvik: "Charu, you did it. You proved that a first-generation

lawyer can make a difference. You've inspired all of us. Keep

fighting, because the world needs more lawyers like you."

Charu smiled as she typed back: "I couldn't have done it without

you. Thank you for believing in me, Satvik. I won't stop now."

As she placed the phone down, Charu closed her eyes, feeling a

deep sense of peace. She had found her purpose, and in doing so,

she had shown the world that with enough determination, anything

was possible.

<u>Chapter 29</u>

Years later, Charu stood before a packed courtroom, addressing a new generation of lawyers. She had become a mentor, a role model for young lawyers who, like her, were just starting out, unsure of their place in a system that seemed stacked against them.

Her words resonated deeply with the room. "I am a first-generation lawyer. I started with nothing but a dream, and I fought for it every step of the way. There were times when I wanted to give up, when the obstacles seemed too great. But I didn't. Because I believed that I could make a difference. And so can you."

Charu looked around at the faces of the young lawyers, and for the first time, she felt a sense of fulfilment. She had not only won her battle but had helped pave the way for others to follow. Her story was one of resilience, of proving that no matter where you come from, or how difficult the journey is, if you keep going, you will find your place in the world.

As she left the courtroom that day, Charu knew one thing for sure: she had made it. And she had made sure that the next generation of lawyers would never feel lost in litigation again.

Chapter 28: The Ripple Effect

Charu's name had become synonymous with perseverance. She had not only emerged victorious in her own battles but had also helped shape the future of law in the country. Her story had been told and retold in legal circles, and young lawyers from all walks of life reached out to her for advice, inspiration, and mentorship. She had become a beacon for those who had always thought that the legal system was out of their reach.

But for Charu, success wasn't measured by the recognition or accolades. It was the moments in between—the quiet victories that no one else saw—that meant the most to her. The letters from young students, the messages from aspiring lawyers, and the gratitude from those whose lives she had touched. Charu knew her true legacy would lie in the impact she had on others, particularly those like her—first-generation lawyers.

One evening, Charu was sitting in her office, a cup of tea in hand, as Dimpu walked in, holding an invitation. It was for the annual law conference, where she had been invited to be the keynote speaker. Charu had spoken at many events before, but this one felt different. The invitation wasn't just a recognition of her legal prowess—it was a testament to the way she had reshaped the narrative for first-generation lawyers.

Dimpu smiled proudly. "Didi, look at this! You're the keynote speaker this year. They want you to inspire the next generation."

Charu chuckled, shaking her head. "I've done nothing more than what any other lawyer would do. I've just had to fight a little harder."

Dimpu sat down next to her. "No, Didi. You've done something incredible. You've shown us that anyone can make it if they believe in themselves, no matter where they come from. You've become the role model that so many of us needed."
Charu smiled softly. "It's not easy, Dimpu. It never was. But it was always worth it. When you're a first-generation lawyer, you face so many doubts—others tell you it's impossible. But all it takes is one person to say, 'I believe in you,' and the world opens up."

At the conference, Charu stood before a crowd of eager faces. Lawyers, students, young professionals—all of them looked up to her as she began her speech. Her journey had been one of struggle, but she was determined to make sure that future generations would not have to fight the same battles.
She began, her voice steady and filled with conviction. "I stand before you today as a first-generation lawyer. There were many times I doubted myself, many times I thought I wasn't cut out for this. But what kept me going was the belief that the law could be a force for good. It could be a tool for justice, not just for the privileged, but for everyone. And that's something worth fighting for."
Charu paused, looking out at the crowd. "To all the young lawyers, especially those from humble beginnings—this journey isn't easy. There will be moments when you want to give up. There will be

times when it feels like you're fighting against the tide. But I promise you, every setback, every struggle, will make you stronger. It will prepare you for the moment when the law needs you the most. The system may seem daunting, but remember, it's only as strong as the people who stand up to protect it."

Satvik was in the audience that day, smiling proudly at his friend. He had been with Charu through every step of her journey. He had witnessed the sleepless nights, the self-doubt, and the eventual triumphs. He knew her better than anyone—Charu wasn't just a lawyer. She was a force of nature, someone who had the ability to inspire and change the world around her.

After the speech, as Charu made her way back to her seat, Satvik caught up with her. "You did it again, Charu. That speech—man, it was incredible. You're giving people hope."

Charu shrugged, a modest smile on her face. "I just told them the truth, Satvik. It wasn't easy, but it was worth it. If even one person walks away thinking, 'I can do this,' then it was worth every sacrifice."

Satvik looked at her with admiration. "You've changed so many lives. And I know you'll keep doing it. There's no stopping you now."

Weeks passed, and Charu's life continued to unfold in ways she had never imagined. Her law firm grew, and she became a mentor to a new generation of young lawyers. She continued to fight cases that mattered, using her platform to speak out against injustice. But her focus was always on those who came after her—first-generation lawyers like herself. She made sure that the doors she had fought so hard to open would remain open for others. Dimpu, now a young law student, often accompanied Charu to various legal events, conferences, and seminars. He had seen his sister's journey firsthand and was determined to follow in her footsteps. Charu's influence on him was profound, and he, too, had set his sights on becoming a lawyer who would make a difference.

One evening, Dimpu sat with Charu at the dinner table, a thoughtful look on his face. "Didi, I've been thinking a lot lately. You've done so much for others, and now I want to do the same. I want to become a lawyer who helps those who don't have a voice. I know it won't be easy, but I'm ready for the fight."

Charu smiled; her eyes filled with pride. "Dimpu, I'm proud of you. But remember, the journey won't always be smooth. There will be times when you'll doubt yourself, when it feels like the world is against you. But just like I did, you'll find a way through it. Keep fighting for what's right. You've got this."

Years later, Charu looked back on her journey and realized that the victories she had won weren't just legal ones. They were personal. The family she had built around her, the community of young lawyers she had inspired, and the countless lives she had touched were the true measure of her success.

Charu had proven that no matter where you came from, no matter how difficult the path, the only thing that mattered was your determination and your willingness to fight for what was right. She had fought her own battle and won. And now, she was ensuring that others would have the opportunity to do the same.

The ripple effect of Charu's journey had just begun. And as she looked out at the world she had helped shape, she knew that the fight for justice would continue—for her, for Dimpu, and for every young lawyer who dared to dream.

The struggle of a first-generation lawyer

The struggle of a first-generation lawyer is marked by numerous challenges, both personal and professional, that require resilience, determination, and unwavering commitment. Here's a summary of the key aspects of their journey:

1. **Lack of Guidance and Support:** First-generation lawyers often come from families without a legal background, which means there's little to no guidance on how to navigate the legal profession. They lack role models or mentors who can provide advice on studying law, finding career opportunities, and overcoming barriers.

2. **Financial Constraints:** Many first-generation lawyers face financial challenges that make pursuing a legal career difficult. Law school fees, study materials, and the costs associated with starting a practice can be overwhelming. Balancing education, internships, and maintaining a livelihood often becomes a huge burden.

3. **Societal Expectations and Pressure:** Coming from a non-legal background, there is often pressure to succeed and prove that entering the legal profession was a worthy

choice. There's also the stigma of not having the family connections that many established lawyers have, making it harder to find opportunities or be taken seriously.

4. **Emotional Struggles and Self-Doubt**: The emotional toll is significant. First-generation lawyers often feel isolated, doubting their own abilities and facing the fear of failure. With no established network, they might feel like outsiders in a profession that traditionally values legacy connections and family ties.

5. **Breaking Stereotypes and Building Trust:** One of the toughest hurdles is earning the trust of clients, peers, and the legal community. Established lawyers, judges, and even clients may question the competence of someone from a non-legal family. First-generation lawyers must work twice as hard to prove their worth.

6. **Establishing a Reputation:** Without the safety net of a family legacy or connections in the field, first-generation lawyers must carve their own path. This often means starting from scratch, building a client base, gaining experience, and establishing a reputation for hard work, integrity, and competence.

7. **Inspiration for Future Generations:** Despite these struggles, first-generation lawyers often become a source of inspiration. By overcoming obstacles, they not only

succeed personally but also pave the way for future generations from similar backgrounds to pursue law. They demonstrate that with dedication, the barriers to entry can be overcome.

In summary, the journey of a first-generation lawyer is filled with numerous challenges, but also immense satisfaction and pride. Through resilience, hard work, and perseverance, they break through the barriers of their circumstances, inspire others, and contribute to a more diverse and equitable legal field.

Here's some advice for first-generation lawyers who are navigating the challenges of entering and succeeding in the legal profession:

1. Believe in Yourself

The first and most important step is self-belief. Doubt will often creep in, especially when you're faced with obstacles that others may not have to deal with. But remember that your unique perspective and determination are powerful assets. You belong in this field as much as anyone else, and your struggles will only make you stronger.

2. Find a Mentor

Seek out mentors who can guide you, even if you don't have family or friends in the legal profession. A mentor can provide valuable advice, introduce you to networks, and help you navigate the complexities of the legal world. Don't hesitate to ask for guidance or advice, and be open to learning from others who have walked the path before you.

3. Network and Build Relationships

Networking is key to success in law. It can be challenging when you don't have family connections in the field, but persistence pays off. Attend legal events, seminars, and conferences, and use social media platforms like LinkedIn to connect with professionals in the industry. Building a supportive network will open up opportunities and offer invaluable resources.

4. Work Hard, But Work Smart

Hard work is essential, but so is working efficiently. Law is a demanding profession, and you'll need to prioritize your time wisely. Be strategic about your studies, your cases, and your career. Focus on continuous learning, whether through formal education, legal training, or simply staying updated on the latest legal developments.

5. Embrace the Journey

There will be setbacks and failures along the way. Don't let them define you. Every challenge you face is an opportunity to learn and grow. Embrace the journey and view every hardship as a stepping stone toward your success. Resilience is often the key to overcoming the toughest obstacles.

6. Be Patient and Persistent

Success doesn't come overnight. It takes time to establish your reputation and build your career. There will be moments when progress feels slow, and you might question whether it's worth it. Stay persistent and trust that your hard work will eventually pay off. The legal field rewards those who are dedicated and consistent.

7. Learn from Your Mistakes

Mistakes are a natural part of the learning process. Don't be afraid to fail, but make sure you learn from every misstep. The ability to adapt and improve is what will ultimately set you apart from others. Being a first-generation lawyer means you'll have to make your own path, and sometimes that requires making mistakes and course-correcting along the way.

8. Build Your Brand

As a first-generation lawyer, you may not have a family name to rely on, but you can still build your own reputation. Focus on demonstrating your expertise, professionalism, and dedication to your clients. Your integrity and the results you deliver will become your brand. Over time, your name will stand for something meaningful in the legal community.

9. Stay True to Your Values

The legal profession can sometimes be challenging in terms of ethics and values. Stay true to your principles and don't compromise your integrity. Uphold honesty and fairness, and remember that your reputation is one of the most valuable things you'll have in your career.

10. Inspire Others

By succeeding as a first-generation lawyer, you're paving the way for others who come from similar backgrounds. Share your story with others, especially those who may doubt their own ability to succeed. You're not just shaping your own future, but you're also inspiring future generations to follow in your footsteps.

11. Take Care of Yourself

Law can be mentally and emotionally taxing. Don't neglect your well-being in the pursuit of success. Make time for self-care, whether that means exercising, meditating, spending time with family, or engaging in hobbies that bring you joy. Maintaining a healthy work-life balance is key to sustaining long-term success in this field.

12. Be Adaptable

The legal field is constantly evolving. Laws change, legal technology advances, and new challenges arise. Stay adaptable and open to new opportunities. Embrace technological tools, stay informed about trends, and be open to learning new skills. Being adaptable will help you remain competitive and successful.

<u>To first-generation lawyers:</u>

Your journey will be difficult, but it will also be incredibly rewarding. Keep pushing forward, and remember that every small step you take brings you closer to your goals. Don't be afraid to dream big and always remember: you're not just building your future—you're also creating opportunities for those who will come after you.

In a world where legacy defines success, Charu dares to challenge the norm. Born into a family with no legal background, she steps into the courtroom armed only with determination, a deep sense of justice, and an unbreakable will. Her sister once dreamed of becoming a lawyer but was forced to sacrifice her ambitions due to life's burdens. Now, Charu carries not just her own dreams, but those of an entire generation longing for change.

From the moment she enters law school, Charu realizes the battle isn't just in the courtroom—it's against the system, societal expectations, and her own doubts. Lacking the connections that many of her peers take for granted, she faces rejection, humiliation, and financial hardships. Yet, every failure fuels her fire.

With the unwavering support of her younger brother, Dimpu, and her motivational friend, Satvik, she learns that success isn't about where you come from, but how fiercely you fight for what you believe in. As she steps into the legal world, battling corruption, injustice, and powerful opponents, Charu's journey transforms from a struggle for survival to an inspiring tale of triumph.

"Lost in Litigation" isn't just a novel—it's a movement. A story for every first-generation lawyer, every dreamer who has been told "no," and every fighter who refuses to give up.

Will Charu prove that passion and persistence can defeat privilege? Will she break through the barriers of the legal elite and establish herself as a force to be reckoned with?

This is not just her fight. This is YOUR fight.

Read "Lost in Litigation" and discover the fire within you.

Thank You.

ABOUT THE AUTHOR

Lucky Singh is a talented young author from Gaya, Bihar, who has taken the literary world by storm with her thought-provoking and inspiring novels. Born and raised in Gaya, Lucky draws inspiration from her humble beginnings and her experiences as a young first-generation lawyer.

Her writing is a reflection of her passion for justice, her love for her hometown, and her admiration for the people who have shaped her life.

Lucky's debut novel, "Captain of My Heart," was a tribute to the life and legacy of Indian cricket legend M.S. Dhoni. The book was a huge success, earning critical acclaim and commercial success. Now, with her second novel, "Lost in Litigation," Lucky has turned her attention to the world of law and justice. Her latest book is a testament to her growth as a writer and her ability to tackle complex themes and issues.

Through her writing, Lucky aims to inspire and motivate young people from small towns and rural areas to chase their dreams and make a difference in the world.

Lucky's writing style is engaging, informative, and thought-provoking. Her characters are well-developed and relatable, and her stories are full of twists and turns that keep readers on the edge of their seats.

With her unique voice and perspective, Lucky Singh is definitely an author to watch out for in the years to come.

Connect with Lucky Singh-: luckysingh2000gaya@gmail.com

Journey of young girl Lucky who find herself in Love With cricket
Legend M.S.Dhoni

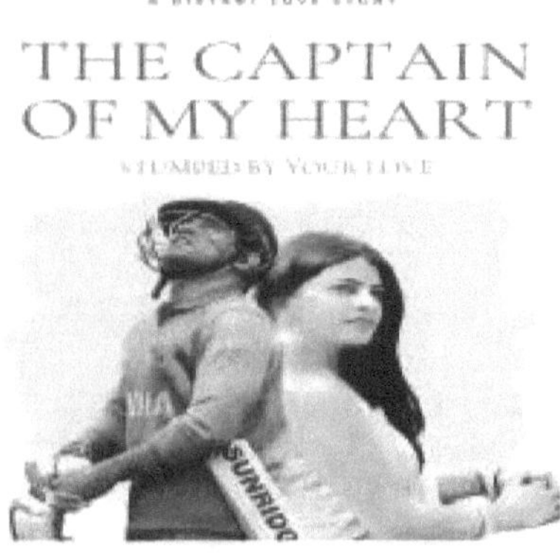

Lucky Singh

Meet Charu a young Firs Generation Lawyer & her inspiring story
is a must-read for anyone interested in Law & Justice.